Shadows and Mysteries: A Collection of Short Stories

Robert Gass

Book Cover by Robert Gass

2024

Contents

Prologue

Stories are like shadows, always present but often unnoticed until the light shifts just so. This collection was born from the spaces in between: the corners of the world where people live their quiet lives, where the extraordinary hides behind the mundane. These tales weave through time and place, capturing moments that resonate with what it means to be human—the ache of loss, the thrill of discovery, the unrelenting search for connection. Each story is a thread, and together they form something intricate, fragile, and unforgettable. Step into the world of these pages, and let the shadows come alive.

This book is more than a collection of short stories; it's a journey through the unexpected. From the hidden lives beneath a city's bridges to the haunting echoes of a long-lost quarry, each story is a glimpse into a world just beyond the veil of the familiar. These tales are deeply personal, born from curiosity, empathy, and an unyielding need to explore the human condition. Writing them was a process of discovery, not just of characters and settings but of the emotions and truths that bind us all. It's my hope that as you read, you'll find pieces of yourself within these pages.

Chapter One

Threads of Yesterday

The wedding dress arrived wrapped in layers of tissue paper, a faint halo of cedar and mothballs trailing it into Emma's workshop. She unwrapped it carefully, peeling back each crinkling sheet like a surgeon exposing fragile skin. The fabric was a pale, bruised ivory, its lace fraying at the edges, but the silhouette was unmistakably exquisite. A dress meant for a storybook bride—or at least one who had lived long enough to become a myth.

The seam that caught her eye wasn't obvious at first. It hid at the hem, a row of crude stitches mismatched against the otherwise perfect craftsmanship. Emma frowned, her fingers brushing the puckered silk. This wasn't the work of the original seamstress. Someone had added it later, the way a secret gets folded into a conversation no one remembers starting.

She fetched her seam ripper, the tool's cool metal a steadying presence in her hand. The stitches came apart reluctantly, the silk fibers sighing as they released their grip. Inside, a small, tightly folded bundle emerged—leather, paper-thin and worn, no larger than the palm of her hand. Emma unfolded it with the care of an archaeologist brushing away centuries of dust.

It was a diary. The ink on its pages had faded to the color of weak tea, but the handwriting was clear: sharp angles and sweeping curves that spoke of a meticulous, determined writer. She read the first line aloud, her voice breaking the stillness of the room.

August 14, 1927.If I can't speak my truth aloud, I'll write it here.

Emma blinked, the words lingering in the air like smoke. She glanced back at the dress, now spread across her worktable, its delicate sleeves limp and lifeless. The story it had carried all these years was suddenly alive, and she couldn't look away.

The diary unfolded like a confession. The writer, M, had poured their heart into its pages, chronicling a love affair as fragile and volatile as the silk of the dress. It began innocently enough: stolen glances across a crowded room, hands brushing in secret, late-night walks by a lake where the moon turned the water into molten silver. The object of M's affection, only referred to as "H," seemed equally captivated, their exchanges brimming with unspoken promises.

But as the entries progressed, the tone darkened. H's letters became sporadic, their meetings rushed and tense. The final pages revealed the bitter truth: H was engaged to someone else, a match arranged for convenience and status. The last entry was dated September 9, 1927:

She said yes. I saw them at the church today, her veil brighter than the sun. He will never love her like I do. He can't. But my love must fit into silence, into shadows, into the hem of this dress.

Emma closed the diary, her chest tight. She stared at the dress, now illuminated by the slanting afternoon light, and wondered if its original owner had ever suspected the secret sewn into its seams.

The next day, Emma called the woman who'd brought her the dress. "I found something," she began, the words catching in her throat. "Inside the hem. It's...a diary."

There was a long pause on the other end. "A diary?" the woman said finally. Her voice was thin, almost hesitant. "Can I come by?"

When the woman arrived, Emma handed her the diary with both hands, as if passing along a fragile artifact. She watched as the woman's expression shifted—first confusion, then recognition, and finally something deeper, a sadness that seemed to settle into her bones.

"This was my grandmother's dress," she said, her fingers tracing the leather cover. "She never spoke much about her wedding day. My mother used to say it was because she didn't believe in looking back. Now I won der..." She trailed off, her gaze distant.

Emma wanted to ask what the woman would do with the diary but stopped herself. Some secrets, even when unearthed, weren't meant to be fully understood.

That evening, as Emma began the meticulous work of repairing the dress, she found herself moving slower than usual. Her needle dipped in and out of the silk, each stitch deliberate, each thread pulling the fabric closer to its original form. But when she reached the hem, she paused. Instead of closing it seamlessly, she left a tiny imperfection—just enough to remind whoever wore the dress next that its beauty had carried more than one story.

And some stories, she thought, were too big to stay hidden.

Chapter Two

When the River Froze

The river froze that winter in a way it hadn't for decades, the ice thick and slick as a promise. I remember it because it was the first time I'd seen the current stop, the water locked beneath its glassy prison. The air carried a silence that seemed unnatural, as though the world itself had paused to see what would happen next.

I was out on the bank, bundled in a coat too thin for the season, casting a line into a hole I'd hacked through the ice. It was the kind of cold that sinks into your marrow, that makes your breath feel like shards in your lungs. Fishing was pointless, really—the perch weren't biting, and I'd already caught enough to fill my small freezer. But sitting there with the rod in my hands gave me something to do, something that felt like purpose.

The first sign of trouble was the sound. A faint cracking, like brittle fingers snapping against each other. At first, I thought it was the ice shifting beneath me. It wasn't until I saw the figure stumbling toward the riverbank that I realized what was happening. He moved like a man on borrowed time, arms flailing, feet slipping on the frost-hardened ground.

"Help!" he called, his voice tearing through the quiet. "Please!"

I dropped my rod and ran, the snow crunching under my boots. He collapsed just as I reached him, a heap of torn wool and raw desperation. His face was gaunt, his skin pale enough to make the blue of his veins stand out. He looked up at me with eyes that were both wild and pleading, and I saw that he was younger than I'd thought—maybe mid-twenties, though the hollows in his cheeks made him look older.

His name was Caleb. He told me this as we huddled in my cabin, a space that barely held the both of us and the heat from the small stove. He'd been trying to cross the river to reach the next town, though what business he had there, he wouldn't say. His coat was soaked through, and I wrapped him in one of my old blankets, the kind with holes worn at the edges but thick enough to keep him from freezing to death.

"You're lucky," I said, pouring him a mug of weak coffee. "Another hour out there, and you'd've been a goner."

He nodded, clutching the mug with both hands like it was the only thing keeping him tethered to the world. "I didn't think anyone would be out there," he said, his voice hoarse. "Thought I was done for."

The days blurred together after that. Caleb stayed, saying the storm had made the roads impassable. I didn't mind the company, though he spoke little and slept less. At night, I'd hear him pacing the small space, his footsteps soft but constant, like he was walking the edge of some great abyss. I asked him once about the marks on his wrists—thin, pale scars that looked deliberate—but he brushed it off, saying only, "They're old. Nothing to worry about."

It wasn't until the third night that he told me about the money. A leather pouch, heavy and bulging, that he pulled from his coat and placed on the table between us. "This is why I was crossing the river," he said, not meeting my eyes. "It's not mine."

He didn't explain further, and I didn't press him. The weight of the pouch seemed to pull the air out of the room, leaving a silence I didn't know how to fill. I went to bed that night with the sound of the ice cracking in my ears, a sound I hadn't noticed since the day I found him.

When the thaw came, Caleb was gone. He left before dawn, taking the pouch and leaving behind only a scrap of paper with a hastily scrawled "Thank you." I didn't expect him to stay, but his absence was like a hole punched through my chest. I spent the morning staring at the river, the ice breaking apart in jagged pieces, each one carried downstream by the rushing water.

It was weeks later when I saw his face again—on the front page of the local paper, under a headline about a bank robbery and a fugitive still at large. The photo was grainy but unmistakable. Caleb, looking straight into the camera with those same wild eyes, like a man who had lived his whole life running.

I think about him often, especially in winter when the river freezes over and the world goes quiet again. I wonder if he ever made it to wherever he was going, or if the ice finally claimed him. I wonder if the money bought him the freedom he seemed so desperate for, or if it only chained him to something worse.

The river keeps its secrets, they say, but I've learned otherwise. It doesn't keep them—it just waits for the right moment to let them go.

Chapter Three

The Watchmaker's Apprentice

Time smelled like oil and brass. It ticked and clicked in the dim corners of the shop, a thousand tiny machines marking moments no one would remember. Levi had spent years among the gears and springs, his fingers nimble and worn from practice but his mind always reaching for something just out of grasp. The old man—they all just called him "Master"—had taught him everything, or at least everything Levi thought there was to know. But he had never spoken of the watch.

The watch was kept in a locked drawer, the key a brass skeleton dangling from a chain around the Master's neck. Levi had asked about it once, early on, when his curiosity still outweighed his fear of the old man's silence. The Master's eyes had flicked to the drawer, then back to Levi, his expression harder than tempered steel. "It's not ready," he'd said, and that was the end of it.

But when the Master died, the shop seemed to exhale its secrets. Levi found the key among the few belongings left behind, its dull gleam a promise he couldn't ignore. The drawer slid open with a groan, revealing the watch nestled in a bed of faded velvet. It was unlike any timepiece he'd ever seen. The case was blackened silver, etched with symbols that looked more like constellations than engravings. The hands moved in a slow, deliberate sweep, but they weren't tracking seconds or minutes. They pointed to something else entirely, something Levi couldn't quite name.

The first time he used it, the world seemed to ripple around him, as if reality were a pond and he'd just dropped a stone into its center. He had turned the dial back a single notch, curious, reckless. One moment, he was in the shop, the scent of warm metal and sawdust thick in the air. The next, he was standing outside, the clock above the town square striking noon, though he knew it had just been half-past.

It felt like power. It felt like control.

But later, when he tried to recall the day's events, there was a gap—a blank space where a memory should have been. It was small, insignificant, the kind of thing most people wouldn't notice. But Levi noticed. He shrugged it off, telling himself it was just fatigue or the strange aftereffects of the watch.

The second time, he didn't shrug it off.

He'd been late for a meeting with the clockmaker's guild, a gathering he couldn't afford to miss if he wanted to keep the shop running. The snow had been heavy that morning, slowing his steps and freezing his breath in the air. He'd turned the watch's dial forward this time, skipping past the trudging walk and arriving at the guild hall in an instant. It worked perfectly. He gave his presentation, his words crisp and his gestures confident, and the guild members nodded in approval.

But when he walked home that evening, the familiar streets seemed foreign. A friend passed him, calling his name, and Levi faltered because he couldn't remember the man's face or how they'd met. It wasn't just forgetting—it was an absence, like the memory had been plucked from his mind and discarded.

The gaps grew wider with each use. He tried to ration it, to only use the watch when it was absolutely necessary, but necessity became a slippery concept. Was it necessary to avoid a painful argument? To skip the agonizing hours spent waiting for news? To relive a fleeting moment of joy? Each time he turned the dial, he told himself it was worth it. Each time, he lost something he couldn't name.

One night, as he sat alone in the shop, the watch heavy in his hands, he turned the dial back as far as it would go. The ripple came, stronger than ever, and he found himself standing in the shop on the day he'd first walked through its doors. The Master was there, his back hunched over a workbench, his hands steady as he adjusted a tiny gear. Levi watched himself enter, a boy of sixteen, wide-eyed and eager. He wanted to reach out, to warn his younger self, to tell him what the watch would cost. But when he tried to speak, no sound came. The scene dissolved around him, and he was back in the present, the watch in his lap and tears streaking his face.

The shop is quiet now. Levi no longer turns the dial, though the temptation never leaves him. He keeps the watch in its velvet-lined drawer, locked away with the same key that once hung around the Master's neck. Some days, he thinks about smashing it, letting its secrets die with him. But then he thinks of the boy who will one day take his place, the apprentice who will inherit the shop and its quiet, ticking mysteries.

And he wonders if the watch will call to them too, or if its toll has finally been paid.

Chapter Four

Salt in the Wound

The sea always had its own voice, a low, guttural murmur that spoke in half-truths and secrets. Martin swore he could still hear it in his sleep, whispering to him like an old, unwanted lover. He had walked away from the water—or tried to—but the ocean never really lets you go. It drags at your ankles, your thoughts, the frayed edges of your dreams. It took years for him to admit that the wreck was the thing he'd been running from, and now here he was, standing on the edge of the dock, salt air clawing at his face like a rebuke.

The boat waiting for him was small and dented, its paint peeling in thin, curling strips. The captain, a wiry man in his sixties, nodded curtly as Martin approached, the kind of nod that said, "I don't ask questions if you don't." That was fine. Martin had no answers to give, not ones that made sense anyway.

The wreck was thirty miles offshore, resting on a sandy plateau about a hundred feet down. The Raven's Fall, they called it, though the name had always felt too poetic for the blunt reality of the place. It was just a steel carcass now, its bones picked clean by the years and the tides. Martin had been there once before, twenty years ago, as a young diver hired to survey the site for artifacts. That was before the accident, before the water turned from familiar to hostile.

The dive had started like any other. Calm seas, good visibility. But something had gone wrong. The currents had shifted suddenly, trapping his partner, Danny, in the wreck's narrow corridors. Martin had tried to save him, fought to pull him free, but the tangle of cables and debris was too much. By the time he surfaced, clutching Danny's empty tank, he was already a ghost.

The present felt thin and fragile as Martin strapped on his gear, the hiss of the oxygen tank loud in his ears. His hands shook as he adjusted the mask, the memory of Danny's voice scraping against his thoughts like barnacles on skin.

"You okay?" the captain asked gruffly, his weathered face unreadable.

Martin nodded, though he wasn't sure it was true. The weight of the gear felt heavier than he remembered, the rubber of the fins stiff and unyielding. He slid into the water, the shock of the cold wrapping around him like a shroud.

Descending was like slipping into another world. The light faded quickly, replaced by an eerie green haze that clung to everything. The wreck loomed into view, its jagged silhouette sharp against the sandy bottom.

Martin's breath echoed in his ears, a metronome counting down the seconds he could endure.

The corridors were narrower than he remembered, their walls coated in algae and rust. He moved carefully, his gloved hands brushing against the steel as if to steady himself. The water pressed against him, a liquid weight that seemed to whisper, "Turn back."

He found the spot easily, though he'd hoped he wouldn't. The narrow passage where Danny had been trapped looked almost untouched, as though time had skipped over it in reverence. Martin crouched, his flashlight sweeping across the debris. He reached out hesitantly, his fingers brushing the edge of a twisted cable.

That's when he saw it: a small, corroded dive knife, half-buried in the sand. It had been Danny's, the initials carved into the handle barely legible through the years of decay. Martin's chest tightened as he picked it up, the weight of it far heavier than the few ounces it should have been.

When he surfaced, the captain was waiting, his eyes scanning Martin's face like he was searching for something. "Find what you were looking for?" he asked, his voice low.

Martin held up the knife, the metal gleaming faintly in the fading sunlight. "Not what I wanted," he said. "But maybe what I needed."

The ride back to shore was silent, the hum of the engine the only sound. Martin stared at the horizon, the knife clutched in his hand. He thought of Danny, of the years he'd spent trying to forget and the moment he'd finally decided to remember. The ocean still whispered to him, but now it sounded different, less like a rebuke and more like a song.

When they reached the dock, Martin stepped off the boat and into the waiting dusk. He slipped the knife into his pocket, its weight a reminder, a promise, a wound that might finally start to heal.

Chapter Five

Voices in the Fog

The fog came in thick that night, rolling over the water like a slow breath exhaled from some unseen mouth. Sam's hands tightened on the ferry wheel, the worn leather grip cool under his fingers. The horn blared, a mournful wail swallowed almost immediately by the dense mist. Beyond the bow, the world disappeared into gray, leaving only the faint shimmer of navigation lights to mark the edge of reality.

Sam had been running the evening route for fifteen years. In all that time, he'd come to expect the peculiarities of the Sound: the way the fog settled in unexpected pockets, how the water's surface could shift from calm to choppy with no warning. But tonight felt different. The air carried a weight that pressed against his chest, and the usual creaks and groans of the boat sounded sharper, like they were protesting something unseen.

And then he heard it.

"Sam."

It wasn't a shout or a whisper, but something in between—a voice carried on the edges of the fog, as if it had been stretched thin by the distance. He froze, his pulse quickening. The deckhand, Charlie, was below with the few passengers, none of whom knew his name. He scanned the empty deck, the shadows of the lifeboats and railings flickering in the weak light.

"Sam."

The voice came again, more insistent this time. It was a woman's voice, soft but edged with something he couldn't place—urgency, maybe, or sorrow. It tugged at him, pulling memories from a place he didn't often visit.

The first time he heard the voice, he told himself it was the wind. By the second and third nights, the excuses felt thinner, like he was trying to patch a sinking boat with strips of duct tape. The voice always came when the fog was heaviest, calling his name from somewhere he couldn't see. It wasn't until the fourth night that he answered.

"Who's there?" he called, his voice steady despite the knot tightening in his throat. The answer came as a laugh, low and broken, a sound that made the hairs on his arms stand on end.

Sam hadn't thought about his grandmother in years. She'd been the one to raise him after his parents drowned when he was eight, a tragedy so tangled in myth and rumor that it had become almost a ghost story itself. The official report said their boat capsized during a storm, but locals whispered about the "fog curse" that had claimed too many lives in the

Sound. His grandmother never spoke of it, not directly. But there had been nights when he'd wake to the sound of her murmuring by the window, staring out at the water with a look that made him shiver.

"They're still out there," she'd said once, her voice barely audible. When he asked who, she'd just shaken her head and said, "You'll know when it's time."

On the fifth night, he saw her.

The fog was so thick that the ferry seemed to float in a void, the water invisible beneath it. He stood on the deck, the voices swirling around him now—not just the woman's, but others, too: low murmurs, faint sobs, the occasional burst of laughter that sounded wrong in the empty night.

And then she appeared. A figure standing at the edge of the bow, her form barely more substantial than the fog itself. She turned, and his breath caught in his throat. It was his mother, her face pale and hollow, her eyes fixed on him with an intensity that burned.

"Sam," she said, her voice the same one that had haunted him for days. "It's time."

He stepped forward, his legs heavy as if the air had thickened around him. "Time for what?" he asked, though he wasn't sure he wanted the answer.

"You need to come back," she said, her words carrying the weight of something final. "You need to remember."

In the days that followed, Sam found himself drawn to the water's edge even when he wasn't working. He pored over old newspapers, searching for details about his parents' deaths, about the "fog curse" and the other disappearances that had plagued the Sound for generations. The pieces began to fit together in a way that made his stomach twist.

The curse wasn't a myth. It was a reckoning, a calling for those who'd been lost to the water to return. And it was his family's legacy.

The final time he heard the voices, he was alone on the ferry. The route had been canceled due to the weather, but he'd taken the boat out anyway, drawn by a need he couldn't explain. The fog swallowed him whole, and the voices rose in a chorus, louder and more urgent than ever.

"Sam."

He stood at the bow, staring into the void, the weight of the years pressing down on him. He didn't speak, didn't move, just let the voices wash over him until one voice rose above the others.

"Come home," it said, and this time, he didn't hesitate.

Sam stepped slowly forward, the fog closing around him like a shroud, and for the first time in years, he felt the weight lift. The ferry drifted on, empty now, the wheel spinning lazily as the water swallowed the last echoes of his name.

Chapter Six

Lanterns on the Water

The river was a silver ribbon under the moonlight, the current slow and steady as it carried the lanterns downstream. Each one flickered like a tiny heartbeat, its soft glow painting the water in shades of gold and amber. People lined the banks, their faces half-lit by the lanterns they'd released moments before, their wishes and prayers written in quick, private scrawls on thin rice paper.

Samantha stood at the edge of the crowd, the damp grass cold beneath her bare feet. She cradled her own lantern carefully, the delicate frame trembling slightly in her hands. The festival had always been her favorite night of the year, a tradition older than anyone in the town could remember. She watched as children darted between the adults, their laughter sharp and bright against the hum of murmured conversations. Somewhere upstream, someone strummed a guitar, the melody floating lazily on the cool night air.

"You going to let it go or just hold it all night?" a voice asked, pulling her from her thoughts. It was Will, his hands shoved deep into the pockets of his worn jacket. His hair was tousled in that deliberate way he never admitted was on purpose, and his smile was equal parts teasing and kind.

Samantha shrugged, her fingers tracing the edges of the lantern's paper. "Maybe I like holding on to it," she said.

Will grinned, leaning closer. "Careful. You hold on too long, and the river might forget you altogether."

She rolled her eyes but stepped closer to the water, the gentle ripples reflecting the stars above. The current felt stronger tonight, or maybe it was just her nerves. With a deep breath, she crouched and set the lantern down, watching as it wobbled for a moment before catching the rhythm of the river. It drifted away, joining the others in a slow, graceful procession toward the horizon.

The first scream came just as the last lantern disappeared from view. It was a sharp, guttural sound that cut through the festival's easy rhythm. People turned, their conversations faltering as a boy, no older than ten, stumbled toward the crowd. He held a lantern in his hands, its light casting jagged shadows across his wide, tear-streaked face.

"It's bad," he gasped, thrusting the lantern forward as though it might burn him. "The message... it says something bad is going to happen."

Samantha's stomach twisted. She pushed through the gathering crowd, her heart pounding. The boy held out the lantern, and she saw the words scrawled on the paper in hurried, uneven letters:

A storm is coming. Run.

In the days that followed, the message became a kind of specter that haunted the town. At first, people dismissed it as a prank, some teenager's idea of a joke. But then the river began to change. The water, usually clear and calm, turned murky and restless. Fish floated belly-up near the shore, their scales pale and bloated. And the air... the air felt different, heavier, like it carried the weight of something unseen.

Samantha couldn't shake the feeling that the message had been meant for her. She spent hours by the river, watching the water churn and listening to the wind whistle through the trees. The festival's joy seemed a distant memory, replaced by a quiet unease that settled over the town like a fog.

"Do you think it's real?" she asked Will one night as they sat on the riverbank, their legs dangling over the edge.

He shrugged, tossing a pebble into the current. "I don't know. But people are scared enough that it might not matter."

"What if it's a warning?" she pressed, her voice barely above a whisper. "What if something..."

Will turned to her, his expression uncharacteristically serious. "If it is, what are you going to do about it?"

The storm came two nights later. It started with the wind, sharp and biting, tearing through the town with a ferocity no one had expected. Rain followed, a relentless downpour that turned roads into rivers and fields into swamps. The river swelled, spilling over its banks and surging toward the town with a force that felt almost sentient.

Samantha ran to the water's edge, her breath coming in ragged gasps. The lanterns, now soaked and crumpled, floated in tangled clusters, their lights extinguished. She scanned the chaos, her heart lurching as she spotted Will, waist-deep in the water, pulling a child onto the shore.

"Will!" she shouted, her voice nearly lost in the roar of the storm. He turned, his face pale and drenched, and gave her a thumbs-up before diving back into the current.

Hours later, when the storm finally passed, the town was left in ruins. Homes were flooded, streets washed out, but no lives were lost. People spoke of the warning with a mixture of awe and fear, wondering who had sent it and why. The river returned to its quiet rhythm, but Samantha knew it would never feel the same again.

Weeks later, as she walked along the water's edge, she found a single lantern caught in the reeds. The paper was damp but intact, the ink smeared but legible. It wasn't a warning this time, but a promise:

We're still watching.

Samantha folded the paper carefully and slipped it into her pocket. The river, it seemed, had more stories to tell.

Chapter Seven

Whispers in the Library

The library smelled of old paper and forgotten time. Dust clung to the air, softening the glow of the flickering overhead light that buzzed faintly like an errant thought. It was the kind of place that whispered to you—not in words, exactly, but in the way the silence seemed to breathe around you, pressing against your skin.

Clara sat hunched at her usual table, her laptop open but untouched. The cursor blinked in time with the ticking clock on the wall, marking minutes she wasn't spending writing. She ran a hand through her hair, her fingers snagging on tangles she'd stopped bothering to comb out. The deadline loomed in her inbox like a silent accusation, but the words wouldn't come. They never came, not the way they used to.

She stared at the bookshelves that rose around her like ancient sentinels. Rows of cracked spines and faded lettering stared back, judging her. She'd come here to escape the noise of her apartment—the drone of her neighbors' TV, the sirens outside her window—but here, in the stillness, the silence felt sharper.

That's when she noticed it. A book on the far shelf, not quite where it should be. It jutted out, just barely, as if someone had left it in a hurry or forgotten to push it back in place. Clara frowned. She'd been in this library enough to know the way its order worked. The librarians were meticulous, almost obsessive, about keeping the shelves pristine. She'd once watched one of them spend twenty minutes re-alphabetizing the biography section.

Curiosity tugged at her like a loose thread. She rose from her chair, her boots scuffing the worn carpet, and made her way to the shelf. The book was old, its spine cracked and its cover bare except for a faded title in gold lettering: Fragments of the Unknown. She pulled it free, her fingers brushing against the brittle pages inside.

The book opened to the middle, as if it had been waiting for her. The words were faint, smudged with time, but she could make out a passage:

The writer stood at the edge of the world, her pen trembling in her hand. The story she carried was not her own, but it clung to her like a second skin.

Clara's breath caught. The words pulled at something deep inside her, something raw and aching. She turned the page, but the next one was blank. So was the one after that. She flipped through the rest of the book in a flurry, but every other page was empty, the faint outline of the first passage the only thing it offered.

"Weird," she muttered, closing the book and sliding it back into place.

When she returned to her table, her laptop screen had gone dark. She tapped the spacebar, the sudden glow making her eyes squint. But as the screen lit up, she froze. The cursor wasn't blinking anymore. Instead, words filled the page, words she hadn't typed:

The writer returned to her table, but the story was already waiting for her.

The books began to move after that. Not in a way that could be seen, exactly, but in the way they rearranged themselves between her visits. A novel she'd never noticed before would appear on the desk where she'd been sitting, its pages dog-eared to passages that mirrored thoughts she hadn't spoken aloud. An atlas, marked with a town she'd dreamed of as a child, sat open on a shelf she swore had been empty the day before.

Clara started coming to the library more often, lingering long after closing time. She'd sit in the shadows, watching as the books seemed to hum with life, their pages fluttering faintly in a breeze that didn't exist. And always, they left her messages—snippets of her own unwritten story scrawled in margins, hidden between lines of text.

One night, she found a journal waiting for her. Its leather cover was worn smooth, its pages blank except for the first line:

What do you need to let go of to tell the truth?

The question lingered in her mind, haunting her as she wrote and rewrote drafts of the novel she couldn't seem to finish. The journal filled slowly, its pages carrying pieces of her she hadn't known were missing.

Memories surfaced—her mother's quiet sighs, her father's stories told in the dark, the way the rain sounded against the roof of the house she'd left behind. The story began to take shape, not from her imagination but from the fragments of herself the library had helped her uncover.

On her final visit, Clara found the library empty. The usual hum of quiet activity was gone, replaced by an almost sacred stillness. She walked to the center of the room, her footsteps echoing softly, and found a single book waiting for her on the main table.

It was her own. The title glinted in the dim light, the pages smooth and crisp as if freshly printed. She opened it to the first page, her breath catching as she read the dedication:

To the library, where I found the pieces I thought I'd lost.

As she closed the book, the lights flickered, and the shelves seemed to sigh in unison. The books were still now, their restless energy spent. Clara walked out into the night, the weight in her chest finally lifting as the story she'd carried for so long found its home.

Chapter Eight

The Cradle of Stars

The observatory stood on the highest hill, its dome a silver eye peering into infinity. Kael spent most nights there, long after the other kids his age had been shooed to bed by their parents. His hands, small but steady, danced over the dials and levers, adjusting the massive telescope's focus with a precision that defied his years. At twelve, he was already a legend among amateur astronomers. The local paper called him "The Sky's Youngest Watchman." Kael hated that nickname, but he didn't hate the sky, he didn't hate the stars.

The sky was everything.

"You'll burn your eyes out staring at that thing," his grandfather had warned, his voice thick with the gravel of a lifetime spent working the docks. Kael had shrugged, his gaze fixed on the faint smudge of the Andromeda galaxy. "Better to burn them out doing something that matters," he'd muttered.

His grandfather's laugh rumbled like distant thunder. "Always the poet, kid. Just like your mother."

Kael's mother had been the one to plant the seed. She was gone now—swallowed by the ocean the same way her mother had been before her. But her stories lingered, trailing Kael like a comet's tail.

"There's a place for us out there," she'd say, pointing to the stars with a finger smudged in charcoal. "One day, we'll find it. Our home among the stars."

She'd tell him about the legend passed down through generations: a celestial event, rare and fleeting, that would guide their family back to their origins. "When the cradle sings," she'd say, "you'll know it's time."

Kael had always thought it was just that—a story. Something to make bedtime feel like an adventure. But as he got older, the words lodged in his chest, growing roots in the quiet spaces between heartbeats.

The night it happened, Kael wasn't looking for anything special. He was mapping exoplanets, his notebook filled with sketches and equations he could barely keep track of. The sky was clear, the kind of clarity that came once or twice a year, when the air felt like glass and the stars were sharp enough to cut.

And then he saw it.

A burst of light, not like the slow crawl of a meteor or the steady pulse of a satellite. This was different. It flared and shimmered, then hung in the sky, pulsing faintly like a heartbeat. Kael's hands moved instinctively, adjusting the telescope's angle, his eye pressed so tightly to the lens it hurt. The object—a nebula, maybe, or something stranger—seemed to ripple with motion, its edges curling inward like petals of an invisible flower.

He scribbled notes furiously, his pen tearing the paper in places. Coordinates, luminosity, approximate size—anything to capture the moment. And then, as quickly as it had appeared, it was gone, swallowed by the dark.

"It's the cradle," Kael said aloud, his voice trembling. He wasn't sure why he believed it, but the certainty rooted itself in him, deep and unshakable.

He spent the next week obsessing over the data, cross-referencing star charts and historical records. His grandfather watched him from the kitchen table, his coffee growing cold as Kael muttered equations under his breath.

"You're gonna drive yourself mad," the old man said one morning, tapping ash from his cigarette into a chipped mug. "Even your mother knew when to let a story be a story."

Kael snapped the notebook shut, his jaw tight. "It's not just a story," he said, his voice cracking. "It's real. I saw it."

The room fell silent, the only sound the faint creak of the wind against the window. His grandfather's eyes softened, and he reached across the table, placing a calloused hand over Kael's. "If anyone can find it, kid, it's you. But don't lose yourself in the trying."

Two weeks later, Kael found himself on the hill again, the observatory's dome glinting in the moonlight. He'd pieced together enough fragments to believe the event wasn't a one-off. It had a cycle, a rhythm, and tonight might be his chance to see it again.

Hours passed. The telescope felt heavier than usual, its mechanisms groaning with each adjustment. Kael's eyes burned from the strain, and he fought the urge to give up, to admit defeat.

And then the sky lit up.

This time, it wasn't just the cradle. The entire swath of stars around it seemed to shift and pulse, forming patterns he couldn't comprehend. It was as if the universe itself were speaking, its voice too vast and ancient for human ears. Kael's chest ached with the weight of it, tears streaming down his face unbidden.

The cradle's light grew brighter, and Kael thought of his mother, of her voice and her stories and the way she'd always believed in things no one else could see. He thought of her words: When the cradle sings, you'll know it's time.

The news broke a month later. Astronomers across the globe confirmed the discovery of a nebula unlike anything seen before, its shape and motion defying existing models. They called it "The Cradle," after Kael's report—a nod to the boy who had spotted it first.

For Kael, the recognition meant little. What mattered was the knowing, the sense of connection that had always eluded him. The stars weren't just distant points of light anymore. They were home, a reminder that he was part of something infinite and enduring.

On quiet nights, when the observatory was empty and the sky stretched endlessly above him, Kael would close his eyes and listen. The cradle's song was faint, but he could still hear it, a melody older than time, guiding him back to where he belonged.

Chapter Nine

The House with Yellow Shutters

The house sat at the end of a gravel road, its yellow shutters faded and cracked like the smile of someone long forgotten. Daniel parked his truck in the overgrown driveway, the weeds brushing against the tires, and stepped out into the cool autumn air. He'd seen the listing in a battered flyer pinned to the bulletin board at the diner. Fixer-upper, must sell. The price was laughably low, even for something that had been sitting empty for a decade.

The front door creaked in protest as he pushed it open. The air inside was stale, tinged with the faint metallic breath of mildew. Dust clung to every surface, turning the light from the grimy windows into hazy beams that stretched across the warped floorboards. It wasn't much to look at, but Daniel had never needed much. Just a project, something to keep his hands busy and his mind from drifting back to the spaces he didn't want to revisit.

The first photograph turned up on the second day. He'd been clearing out the upstairs bedroom, its walls still papered with faded roses, when he found the box tucked beneath the bed. It was wooden, the lid warped and splintered, as though someone had tried to pry it open in a hurry. Inside were stacks of black-and-white photos, their edges yellowed and brittle.

The first image stopped him cold. It was a man, standing in front of a house. This house. The shutters behind him were freshly painted, the color bright and cheerful. The man had the kind of face that made you think of words like reliable or steadfast. But what made Daniel's chest tighten was the way the man looked—the slope of his shoulders, the slight tilt of his head. It was like looking in a mirror warped by time.

By the third week, the photographs felt like an obsession. Each one he found told a fragment of a story, but the pieces didn't fit together neatly. There was the man again, standing with a woman who wore a floral dress and a smile that didn't quite reach her eyes. Another photo showed the two of them holding a baby, the man's expression unreadable. And then there were the stranger ones—images of empty rooms with shadows that didn't belong, or the man staring out of a window that no longer existed.

The photos weren't just eerie; they felt personal, like someone had been documenting a life Daniel hadn't yet lived. He'd find himself staring at them late into the night, the faint hum of the space heater the only sound in the empty house. Each photo seemed to whisper a question he couldn't answer.

"You okay, man?" his friend Marcus asked one afternoon, standing in the gutted kitchen. Marcus had stopped by to help with the plumbing, but Daniel hadn't picked up a wrench all day.

"Yeah," Daniel said, his voice flat. He gestured toward the stack of photographs on the counter. "Just trying to make sense of these."

Marcus flipped through the top few, his brow furrowing. "Weird. Where'd you find them?"

"Here," Daniel said. "In the house. It's like... it's like they were waiting for me."

Marcus snorted. "You've been spending too much time alone out here. They're just old photos. Probably belonged to whoever lived here before."

Daniel nodded, but the explanation didn't sit right. The faces, the moments captured in the photographs—they felt too deliberate, too connected to him.

The last photograph appeared two months later, the day Daniel decided to tear out the old closet in the main bedroom. It was wedged behind a loose board, the paper stiff and brittle as though it had been waiting there for years. The image showed the man again, standing in front of the house. But this time, the shutters were faded and cracked, just like they were now. And in the background, barely visible through the dusty lens, was Daniel himself, standing at the window, watching.

He dropped the photograph, his breath catching in his throat. It couldn't be real. It was a trick of the light, a flaw in the image. But no matter how many times he picked it up, stared at it, tried to rationalize it, the figure in the window didn't change.

Daniel stopped working on the house after that. The tools sat untouched in the corner, the walls half-painted. He couldn't explain it, but the air felt different, heavier, as though the house itself was holding its breath. The nights grew longer, the shadows in the corners darker. He started hearing things—the faint creak of footsteps on the stairs, the distant sound of laughter that stopped the moment he strained to hear it.

The house wasn't just a place anymore. It was a presence, one that seemed to know him better than he knew himself.

On the final night, Daniel packed a bag and left. As he drove down the gravel road, he didn't look back, didn't glance at the house with its yellow shutters standing silent against the horizon. But he knew, without question, that it was watching him leave.

And somewhere inside, waiting to be found, another photograph lay hidden, its edges curling with time, ready to tell the next part of the story.

Chapter Ten

Shadows in the Orchard

The orchard stretched over the rolling hills like a green quilt, the trees heavy with fruit that smelled of sunlight and damp earth. Arturo wiped his brow with the back of his hand, the sticky sweetness of the apples clinging to his skin. The sun hung low, painting the horizon in streaks of amber and rose, but there was still work to be done. There was always more work.

"Arturo!" Luis called from the next row, his voice sharp and teasing. "You're slower than my grandmother! We're supposed to finish this row before sundown."

Arturo rolled his eyes, straightened his back, and hefted the wicker basket onto his hip. "Your grandmother would probably pick faster than you," he shot back. Luis's laughter echoed through the orchard, warm and familiar.

The air cooled as the sun dipped lower, the shadows between the trees growing longer and darker. Arturo moved methodically, his hands plucking apples with practiced ease, when something caught his eye. A patch of bark, smooth and pale against the rough trunk of a tree. He stepped closer, curiosity tugging at him, and saw the initials carved deep into the wood: M.H. + J.L.

The letters were neat, precise, as though whoever had made them had taken their time. They were old, the edges softened by years of growth, but still clear enough to read. Arturo ran his fingers over them, the grooves cool beneath his touch.

"Luis," he called, his voice quieter now. "Come look at this."

"It's probably just some teenagers messing around," Luis said, leaning on his basket as he inspected the carving. But there was something in his tone—something hesitant, almost uneasy—that made Arturo press further.

"They're old," Arturo said. "And look at how deep they are. That wasn't done with a pocketknife. Someone cared about this."

Luis shrugged, but his eyes darted toward the distant farmhouse where the foreman lived. "There's stories about this place, you know. My dad said a girl went missing here years ago. Back in the '70s, I think. Nobody ever found her."

The words settled heavily between them. Arturo glanced back at the tree, the initials suddenly taking on a weight they hadn't carried before.

That night, Arturo couldn't sleep. The image of the carving stayed with him, vivid and unrelenting. He thought of the orchard, how its beauty felt endless during the day but turned unfamiliar and secretive under the cover of darkness. He thought of the girl Luis had mentioned, her name and story lost to time, and felt a strange pull to know more.

The next morning, Arturo went to the farmhouse. The foreman, Mr. Harper, was on the porch, a cigarette dangling from his lips. He looked up as Arturo approached, his weathered face unreadable.

"What can I do for you, kid?" Harper asked, exhaling a thin stream of smoke.

Arturo hesitated, then blurted, "I found something in the orchard. Initials carved in a tree. Do you know anything about them?"

Harper's expression didn't change, but his eyes darkened. He took a long drag from his cigarette before answering. "A lot of people've worked that orchard over the years. Plenty of initials carved, plenty of stories told. Nothing ever comes of it."

"Luis said a girl went missing here," Arturo pressed. "Do you know her name?"

For a moment, Harper said nothing. Then he stubbed out his cigarette on the porch railing and stood. "You're better off leaving it alone. Some things are meant to stay buried."

Arturo didn't leave it alone. He spent his evenings at the library, poring over old newspapers and town records. It took weeks, but he found her. Maria Hernandez. Sixteen years old, last seen picking apples in the orchard. She'd been wearing a blue dress. Her boyfriend, James Lathrop, had been the last person to see her, but he'd disappeared shortly after she did. The case had gone cold, the whispers fading into the town's collective memory.

The initials made sense now. M.H. + J.L. Maria and James.

It was late October when Arturo went back to the tree. The air was sharp, the kind that carried the promise of frost. He stood beneath the branches, the wind rustling the leaves above him, and ran his fingers over the carving again.

"What happened to you?" he whispered, the words swallowed by the stillness around him.

The ground beneath the tree felt softer than it should have, the soil loose and uneven. Arturo frowned, crouching down and digging with his hands. The earth gave way easily, and soon he uncovered something hard, wrapped in decaying fabric. His breath caught as he pulled it free, revealing a rusted tin box.

Inside were scraps of paper, a photograph, and a locket. The photo showed a girl in a blue dress, her arm wrapped around a boy with a shy smile. Maria and James. The papers were love letters, their ink faded but legible, filled with promises of escape and devotion. And the locket... the locket held a lock of dark hair, coiled like a question that would never be answered.

Arturo sat back on his heels, the box heavy in his lap. The orchard stretched out around him, quiet and endless, but it didn't feel the same. It felt like it was watching, holding its breath.

He didn't tell Harper about the box. He didn't tell Luis. Some stories, Arturo realized, weren't meant to be solved. Some shadows were better left in the orchard.

Chapter Eleven

A Song for the Broken

The city had its own rhythm, a cacophony of car horns, distant sirens, and the shuffle of footsteps on cracked pavement. Alex knew it well, had lived in it, played in it, and bled in it. His corner—the one just past the diner with the flickering neon sign—was his stage, his sanctuary. The battered guitar case, held together by duct tape and hope, sat open in front of him, coins and crumpled bills scattered like confessions.

He played for the ones who stopped. The woman with the mismatched socks who always hummed along. The construction worker who nodded in time with the beat. The kid who danced like no one was watching. His songs weren't polished or perfect, but they were his. Raw and real, strung together from frayed chords and the stories he carried in his head and in his heart.

The tape appeared on a Thursday, in the kind of weather that makes the world feel waterlogged. Alex's fingers were stiff from the cold, the strings biting into his skin. He'd just finished playing when he saw it, lying next to his case, half-hidden under a tattered flyer for a missing cat. An old cassette tape, the label faded but legible: *For the Broken.*

He picked it up, turning it over in his hands. The plastic was scratched, the reels inside still intact. No name, no track list. Just those three words scrawled in handwriting that tilted slightly to the left. He looked around, but the crowd had thinned, faces disappearing into the rain.

The pawn shop smelled like dust and despair. Alex walked in, the cassette clutched in his jacket pocket, and nodded to Sal, who stood behind the counter reading a yellowed paperback.

"Need a player," Alex said, pulling the tape out and placing it on the counter.

Sal raised an eyebrow, glancing at the cassette. "Haven't seen one of these in years. Thought you'd gone all digital."

"Found it. Don't even know what's on it."

Sal grunted and disappeared into the back, returning with a dusty Walkman and a pair of foam-padded headphones. "Ten bucks," he said, and Alex handed over the crumpled bills from his guitar case.

The melody hit him like a gut punch. It started slow, a single haunting note that hung in the air, vibrating with something he couldn't name. Then the chords came, layered and complex, weaving a soundscape that felt both foreign and familiar. By the time the voice entered—a low, gravelly whisper that carried the weight of a thousand heartbreaks—Alex was frozen.

He listened to the tape over and over that night, each replay peeling back another layer. The lyrics were a mosaic of pain and longing, of loss and redemption. And yet, there was hope buried in the sound, a faint light flickering in the shadows.

The search began the next day. Alex asked everyone he knew—Sal, the barista at the coffee shop, the old man who played saxophone two blocks down. No one recognized the music. It wasn't on any streaming service, didn't match any band or artist Alex could name. It was as though the tape had materialized out of thin air.

But Alex couldn't let it go. He started playing pieces of the melody on his corner, weaving it into his own songs. People stopped more often, their faces open and raw, as if the music was speaking to something buried deep inside them. The woman with the mismatched socks began crying one afternoon, her tears falling silently as Alex played.

"Where did you hear that?" she asked, her voice trembling.

Alex paused, his fingers hovering over the strings. "Found it on a tape. You know it?"

She shook her head, wiping her eyes. "No, but it feels like I should."

Weeks turned into months. The tape became an obsession, a thread Alex couldn't stop pulling. He visited record stores, trawled online forums, even put up flyers asking for information. Each lead fizzled into nothing, but the music stayed with him, growing louder in his mind until it was all he could hear.

One night, while playing a late set, a man approached him. He was older, his hair streaked with gray, and he carried a guitar case that looked as worn as Alex's.

"The song," the man said, his voice rough. "Where did you hear it?"

Alex's heart leapt. "It was on a tape. Found it a few months ago. Do you know it?"

The man nodded slowly, his eyes distant. "I wrote it. Years ago. For my son."

Alex stared at him, the pieces clicking into place. "What happened?"

The man's hands tightened around the handle of his guitar case. "He was broken. Couldn't find his way out. I wrote the song hoping it would reach him, but it was too late."

Alex didn't know what to say. The weight of the man's words settled over him, heavy and unyielding. Finally, he pulled the tape from his pocket and handed it over. "It reached me," he said quietly. "And a lot of others too."

The man took the tape, his fingers trembling. For a long moment, neither of them spoke. Then he nodded, his eyes glistening. “Thank you,” he said. “For keeping it alive.”

Alex kept playing the song, even after the man disappeared back into the city’s shadows. He played it for the broken, for the lost, for the ones searching for something they couldn’t name. And in its melody, he found his own way back, one note at a time.

Chapter Twelve

The Glass Menagerie

The furnace roared like a living thing, its heat pressing against Lydia's face as she worked the molten glass with a rod that felt almost weightless in her practiced hands. Her studio was a cavern of light and shadow, the walls lined with shelves that gleamed with her creations. Animals caught mid-stride, bowls that seemed to breathe with their own color, delicate flowers that could shatter with a sigh—each piece a fragment of her, fragile and enduring.

She preferred working at night, when the town slept and the world outside her windows dulled to a quiet hum. There was no need to explain herself then, no curious eyes peering into her solitude. She could create in silence, her thoughts and the rhythm of her craft the only company.

It was on a night like this, a week after the dream, that she noticed the first one.

The dream had been vivid, more so than usual. She stood in a field of silver grass under a sky that shimmered with a thousand shifting hues. At its center was a stag, its antlers like frozen lightning, its body so luminous it seemed to pulse with its own heartbeat. When it turned its head to look at her, she woke with a start, her breath catching as though she'd been running.

The memory lingered throughout the day, the image of the stag etched into her mind. That evening, without knowing why, she found herself working the glass into the shape of the animal. The antlers were the hardest part, each tine needing to curve just so, delicate but strong. By dawn, it stood finished on her workbench, its form perfect in a way that unsettled her.

She didn't notice the light inside it until the next evening. The stag sat on her shelf, its body catching the faint glow of the furnace, and as she passed by, she saw it—a faint pulse, like the memory of a heartbeat. She stepped closer, her fingers trembling as she reached out to touch it. The light flickered once, then disappeared, leaving her staring at her own distorted reflection in the glass.

It didn't stop with the stag. Night after night, she dreamed, and night after night, her hands shaped the visions into form. A flower with petals like the scales of a dragon. A ship caught in a tempest, its sails frozen mid-tatter. A child's face, half-hidden in shadow, with eyes that seemed to follow her. Each piece held something of the dream, something that felt alive.

She tried to ignore it at first, chalking it up to the tricks of an overworked mind. But the light inside the glass wouldn't let her. It came and went without warning, faint and fleeting, like a memory trying to surface. And always, the pieces seemed to watch her, their presence too weighty for mere objects.

The dreams grew darker. She found herself in places that felt wrong, their edges too sharp or too blurred. A forest where the trees whispered her name. A shoreline where the tide pulled away, leaving the sand littered with broken mirrors. A room that looked like her studio, except the shelves were bare, and her hands held nothing but ash.

One night, she dreamed of a figure standing at the edge of her furnace's glow. It was tall, its face obscured by shadow, and it held one of her creations in its hand. When it turned toward her, she woke with a start, the air in her room cold despite the summer heat.

The next morning, she found the glass stag shattered on the floor.

She stopped working for a time, the furnace left cold and silent. The shelves gathered dust, and the studio became a place she avoided. But the dreams didn't stop. If anything, they became more insistent, their images pressing against her mind like hands against glass. She woke each morning feeling hollow, as though the dreams were stealing pieces of her.

One night, unable to bear the weight of it any longer, she returned to the studio. The furnace roared to life, its light filling the space like an old friend. She pulled out the tools she'd abandoned and set to work, her hands moving with a purpose she didn't fully understand.

This time, she didn't try to shape the dream. She let it guide her, her fingers working the glass into a form she couldn't see until it was finished.

When she stepped back, her breath caught. It was a window, its frame delicate and intricate, the glass within rippled like water. And in its surface, she saw the dreams—not as fragments, but as a whole.

The stag stood in the field. The ship braved the tempest. The forest whispered, and the tide pulled away. And at the center of it all was the figure, standing in the glow of her furnace, holding her creations in its hands.

The light inside the window pulsed once, then faded. Lydia stared at it, her reflection and the dreams merging into one. She didn't know what it meant, or why it had chosen her, but for the first time in months, the weight inside her chest lifted.

The furnace burned through the night, and when the dawn came, Lydia's shelves were no longer empty.

Chapter Thirteen

Strangers on the Tracks

The train had stopped hours ago, its wheels frozen in place somewhere between Nowhere and Forgettable. Outside the window, the landscape was an endless smear of gray, the sky heavy with the threat of rain that couldn't be bothered to fall. Inside, the air was stale with the mingling of too many people and too few open windows. Conversations were murmured and sparse, the kind of aimless chatter that only filled the void of time when everyone knew there was nothing else to do.

Emily sat in seat 23B, her head against the cold glass, trying to will herself into a nap that wouldn't come. The book she'd brought lay abandoned on her lap, the words blending into a blur she couldn't focus on. Across from her, a man with sharp features and a scuffed leather jacket tapped his foot to a rhythm only he could hear. He looked up, catching her eye, and offered a faint smile that lingered somewhere between awkward and polite.

“Hell of a delay,” he said, his voice rough like gravel underfoot.

Emily nodded, unwilling to engage but too polite to ignore him completely. He leaned back in his seat, arms crossed, his foot still tapping.

“I’m Jack,” he added after a moment, as though the silence had goaded him into action.

She hesitated, then sighed. “Emily.”

“Nice to meet you, Emily. You headed somewhere interesting?”

“Boston,” she said, her tone clipped. “Work.”

Jack’s eyebrows lifted slightly, but he didn’t press her further. Instead, he turned his gaze toward the window, his reflection faint and ghostlike against the dim view.

The hours dragged on. The train jerked once, as if it might lurch forward, but then settled back into its sullen stillness. Emily found herself watching Jack out of the corner of her eye. He pulled a battered notebook from his bag and began to scribble, his handwriting slanted and uneven. The curiosity finally won out.

“What are you writing?” she asked.

Jack looked up, surprised. He held the notebook out toward her but didn’t hand it over. “Just thoughts. Random stuff. Helps pass the time.”

Emily smirked. "Deep thoughts, or grocery lists?"

"A little of both." He flipped a page, showing her a sketch of a bridge, half-finished but detailed enough to recognize. "I'm an architect," he said, by way of explanation. "Or at least, I used to be."

"Used to be?"

Jack shrugged, his expression closing off. "Took a break. Needed some distance."

Emily nodded, recognizing the weight in his voice. She glanced at her own reflection in the glass, thinking of the years she'd spent running from one thing or another, always calling it something else—an opportunity, a new challenge, never an escape.

The conversation trickled back to life over the next hour. Jack talked about the bridges he'd designed, the cities he'd lived in. Emily shared pieces of her own story—the marketing job she didn't love but didn't hate, the apartment she rented but didn't call home. They talked about music and books, the kind of aimless topics that felt safe but somehow edged closer to something real.

And then Jack asked a question that changed everything.

"Do you believe in coincidences?"

Emily frowned, caught off guard. "I guess? Why?"

Jack hesitated, his fingers drumming against the armrest. "It's just... you remind me of someone."

Emily's stomach tightened. "Who?"

"My sister," he said quietly. "I lost her years ago. She... she would've been about your age now."

Emily felt the words settle heavily between them, and for a moment, she didn't know what to say. "I'm sorry," she managed, her voice soft.

Jack shook his head. "It's fine. It was a long time ago. But it's weird, you know? Seeing someone and thinking they could've been part of a life you'll never get back."

Emily swallowed hard, the weight of his words pressing against her own memories. "I know what you mean," she said, surprising herself. "My brother... he died when I was twelve. I don't think I ever really dealt with it."

Jack's eyes met hers, something unspoken passing between them. The train felt smaller in that moment, the shared silence heavier than the din of the stranded passengers.

When the train finally lurched back to life, the sun was setting, casting long shadows across the cabin. Emily and Jack sat quietly, their conversation ebbing into a comfortable silence. As the train pulled into the station, Jack stood, slinging his bag over his shoulder.

"Take care, Emily," he said, his voice warm.

She nodded, watching as he stepped off the train and disappeared into the crowd. It wasn't until she'd left the station herself, her bag slung over her shoulder, that she realized he'd left his notebook behind.

Inside, on the last page, was a sketch of a bridge. And beneath it, a name she hadn't spoken aloud in years: "Charlie."

Her brother's name.

Emily stared at the page, her breath catching. The world seemed to shift around her, the past and present colliding in a way she couldn't explain. She clutched the notebook to her chest, the weight of it grounding her as she stepped into the fading light, the city alive with possibility.

Chapter Fourteen

The Horizon Never Ends

The ocean had a way of making you feel small. Not in the humbling, poetic sense, but in the way it erased you, piece by piece. Out there, with nothing but the hiss of waves against the hull and the groan of the wind in the rigging, you became little more than a dot on an endless, shifting map. For Mark, that was the point.

He'd left the marina two weeks ago, a quiet departure with no one there to wave him off. The Solitude, his thirty-two-foot sloop, was his entire world now, its fiberglass hull a fragile shell against the immensity of the Pacific. He wasn't running from anything, or at least that's what he told himself. It wasn't about escape. It was about freedom. About finding something he couldn't name.

The days blurred together in a rhythm of salt and sun. He woke with the dawn, checked his bearings, and set the sails to catch the faintest whisper of wind. Nights were harder, the darkness pressing against him like a weight. The radio was his only tether to the outside world, its static-filled updates a reminder that somewhere beyond the horizon, life went on.

It was on the eleventh night that he first heard it. He was tuning through frequencies, hoping for a weather report, when a voice crackled through the static. Faint, distorted, but unmistakable.

"...and the stars, they shine brighter tonight. You're listening to Horizon Radio, keeping you company wherever you roam."

Mark froze, his hand hovering over the dial. The voice was warm, almost musical, with an accent he couldn't place. He leaned closer, straining to catch every word.

"Out here, we're all just drifters, aren't we? But remember, no matter how far you go, the horizon never ends."

And then, music. A haunting melody, low and resonant, like something pulled from a dream. Mark sat back, his pulse quickening. He'd scanned these frequencies a dozen times before and never heard anything like it.

The signal came again the next night, and the night after that. Each time, the same voice, the same strange, otherworldly music. Mark tried to pinpoint the source, triangulating coordinates based on the signal strength, but the numbers didn't make sense. According to his calculations, the broadcast was coming from the middle of the ocean—a place where no station should exist.

He began staying up later, his eyes gritty with exhaustion, waiting for the voice to return. It always did, just past midnight, filling the cabin with its calm, hypnotic rhythm. The voice spoke of stars and tides, of journeys and destinations, its words laced with a peculiar kind of wisdom that made Mark's chest ache.

"To the sailor out there wondering if he's lost... you're not. You're exactly where you need to be."

Mark's hands tightened on the radio. "Who are you?" he whispered, though he knew the signal couldn't hear him.

By the fifteenth day, Mark's curiosity had morphed into obsession. He charted a course toward the coordinates he'd calculated, pushing the Solitude harder than he should have. The waves grew choppier, the wind more capricious, but he didn't care. The voice had become a beacon, a thread he couldn't let go of.

The storm came without warning. One moment, the sky was clear; the next, it was a seething mass of black clouds and howling wind. The Solitude pitched violently, water cascading over the bow as Mark fought to keep the sails under control. The radio crackled to life, the voice cutting through the chaos.

"Hold steady, sailor. The storm will pass."

Mark laughed, a bitter, desperate sound. "Easy for you to say," he muttered, his grip white-knuckled on the tiller. But the voice was right. After what felt like hours, the storm began to abate, the wind easing and the waves softening into gentle swells.

When the sun rose, the ocean was eerily calm. Mark collapsed onto the deck, his body aching, his mind a jumble of exhaustion and relief. He closed his eyes, the hum of the radio still faintly audible in the background.

He woke to find the horizon empty. No land, no ships, nothing but water stretching endlessly in every direction. He checked his charts, his GPS, but they offered no answers. According to his instruments, he was somewhere that didn't exist.

The radio crackled again, and this time, the voice was clearer than ever.

"Welcome, sailor. You've found us."

Mark's heart pounded. "Who are you?" he asked aloud, his voice hoarse.

The silence stretched, and then the voice replied, soft and knowing. "We're the ones who listen. The ones who wait. And now, you're one of us."

The music began again, wrapping around him like a tide, pulling him into its rhythm. Mark closed his eyes, the horizon fading as the sound carried him somewhere he couldn't name.

Chapter Fifteen

The Keeper of the Keys

The key ring clinked softly with every step, a muted chime that accompanied Walter through the cavernous halls of the museum. He'd been the janitor here for twenty-six years, long enough to know every corner, every creak, every display case that needed its glass wiped just so to avoid streaks under the lights. The keys, heavy and worn smooth from decades of use, were his constant companions. They opened doors, locked up secrets, and, in Walter's mind, carried the stories of all the hands they'd passed through.

On most nights, the museum was his alone. The visitors were gone, their chatter and footsteps replaced by the soft hum of the HVAC and the occasional echo of distant street noise. It was Walter's favorite time, the exhibits standing silent and watchful, as though they, too, were resting.

It was on a quiet Thursday evening, while mopping near the Egyptian gallery, that he noticed it. One of the keys, smaller and older than the others, seemed to catch the faint light differently, its brass surface almost glowing. Walter paused, the mop handle steady in his grip, and stared at the key. He couldn't recall ever using it.

Curiosity tugged at him, and before he could think better of it, he unhooked the key and turned toward the gallery's locked storeroom. The door was ancient, its wood scarred with time, and the key slipped into the lock as though it belonged there. With a hesitant turn, the mechanism clicked, the sound unusually loud in the quiet hall.

Inside, the air was thick with the scent of age—dust, parchment, something faintly exotic. The room was cluttered with artifacts that hadn't made it to the displays: broken pottery, faded textiles, an odd assortment of tools and trinkets. But what caught Walter's eye was the mirror.

It stood in the corner, its frame ornate and gilded, vines and flowers carved into the wood. The glass itself was clouded, its surface rippling slightly like water caught in a breeze. Walter approached it slowly, his r-eflection wavering and indistinct. He reached out, his fingers brushing the cool surface, and suddenly, the room shifted.

The storeroom was gone. Walter was outside, standing in a bustling marketplace. The air was warm and alive with sound: the clatter of hooves on cobblestones, the sing-song voices of merchants hawking their wares, the laughter of children darting between stalls. He looked down at his hands, still holding the key ring, and then back at the mirror, which now stood freestanding in the middle of the square.

It was the same place, the same frame, but through it, he could see the storeroom—a window back to where he'd come from. Walter's heart raced as he realized what had happened. The key hadn't just unlocked the door. It had unlocked the past.

Over the next few weeks, Walter experimented with the key. Each door he opened brought him to a different moment in time, tied to the artifacts in the museum. Through a display case in the Victorian wing, he watched a craftsman meticulously carve the very clock that now sat behind the glass. In the natural history gallery, a locked cabinet revealed a prehistoric jungle, the air humid and teeming with life.

Each journey was breathtaking, but it was the people who stayed with him. A young girl in 18th-century Paris, carefully painting porcelain plates while humming a tune he didn't recognize. A soldier in a World War I trench, his hands shaking as he read a letter by candlelight. Their lives, their moments, felt as vivid as his own, and Walter found himself thinking about them long after he returned to the present.

But the key had rules. The past could be observed but not changed. Walter learned this the hard way when he saw a fire break out in a 19th-century factory. He shouted, waved his arms, tried to warn the workers, but his voice fell flat, his presence unseen. All he could do was watch as the flames consumed the building, the heat licking at his skin even as he stood helpless in the middle of it all.

The guilt stayed with him, heavy and unshakable. He began to wonder if he should stop using the key, if knowing these stories but being powerless to alter them was more burden than gift. But then he found the diary.

It was in the Renaissance gallery, inside a locked chest beneath a display of illuminated manuscripts. The diary was bound in cracked leather, its pages filled with careful, looping script. Walter flipped through it, stopping at a passage dated June 14, 1547:

To the one who holds the keys: You are not the first, and you will not be the last. We are keepers of stories, stewards of the moments that define us. The past is not yours to change, but it is yours to carry. Do so with care.

Walter stared at the words, the weight of them settling over him. The key wasn't about power or control. It was about remembering, about bearing witness. And maybe, in some way, that was enough.

Now, when Walter walks the museum at night, the key ring still clinks softly at his side. He doesn't open the doors as often as he used to, but when he does, he treats the moments he finds with reverence. The past may be out of reach, but its echoes linger, reshaping the way he sees the present.

In the quiet halls of the museum, Walter knows he's not just a janitor anymore. He's a keeper of the keys, a guardian of time, and the stories he carries are etched into him as surely as the grooves on the brass.

Chapter Sixteen

Ashes in the Wind

The forest smelled like smoke and sorrow. Even days after the wildfire had been declared "under control," its ghosts lingered in the charred remains of what had once been a thriving ecosystem. Grayson walked the scorched earth, his boots crunching over brittle remnants of branches, his breath heavy in the still, acrid air. He was used to this—the aftermath, the silence—but it never stopped feeling like a kind of loss.

He spotted it near the remnants of a cluster of pines, their trunks blackened and skeletal. The urn was half-buried in ash, its metallic surface dull but intact. Grayson crouched, brushing away the soot with a gloved hand. It was simple, unadorned except for a faint engraving near the base: *L.L.*

For a moment, he just stared at it. He'd found strange things in the aftermath of fires before—melted car keys, scorched photo albums, even a porcelain doll with its face cracked but still eerily intact. But this was different. This was personal.

He picked it up, feeling the unexpected weight of it, and turned it over in his hands. The lid was sealed, though the fire had left scorch marks along its edges. Grayson's chest tightened. Who had left this here, and why?

The park office was quiet that afternoon, the usual bustle of hikers and campers replaced by the low hum of a fan struggling against the lingering heat. Grayson placed the urn on his desk, its presence both incongruous and commanding. He ran his fingers through his hair, trying to piece together what little he knew.

"Find something interesting out there?" Casey asked, leaning against the doorway. She was another ranger, her uniform as dusty and sweat-streaked as his own. Her tone was light, but her eyes were curious.

Grayson gestured toward the urn. "Found this in the burn area. Near Pine Hollow."

Casey's brows furrowed as she stepped closer. "An urn? That's... unusual."

"Yeah," Grayson said, his voice quieter now. "Thought it might be worth looking into. Maybe someone... lost it."

Casey gave him a look, one that hovered between skepticism and concern. "You're not going to let this go, are you?"

Grayson shook his head. "No. I'm not."

The first clue came from the engraving. Grayson spent the evening poring over records, both local and online, searching for any connection to the initials L.L. paired with an urn. He called funeral homes, crematoriums, even the local historical society, but the answers were sparse, the trail cold.

It wasn't until he found a forgotten article buried in the archives of the town's newspaper that the pieces began to take shape. Lorraine Langston, 72, beloved teacher and lifelong resident, passed away peacefully last year. Her ashes were entrusted to her family for scattering in her favorite place: Pine Hollow.

Grayson stared at the screen, the words blurring as a wave of understanding settled over him. Lorraine Langston. L.L. Her family had brought her here, to the place she loved, and then the fire had come. The ashes scattered in a final, chaotic gesture, leaving only the urn behind.

He found the Langston family's number in the phone book, a relic that still clung to life in their small town. When he called, a woman answered, her voice cautious but kind.

"This might sound strange," Grayson began, his words careful, "but I think I found something that belongs to you. An urn."

There was a pause on the other end of the line, the kind of silence that stretched long enough to feel like a question. Then the woman spoke, her voice tight with something between relief and grief. "That was my mother's. We... we thought it was lost. After the fire, we couldn't find it."

"I'd like to return it," Grayson said, his tone soft. "If that's okay."

"Yes," the woman said quickly. "Please. Thank you."

The Langston home was modest, its porch adorned with flower pots that had seen better days. The woman who answered the door—Lila, Lorraine's daughter—looked tired but grateful. She took the urn from Grayson with trembling hands, holding it close as though it were a part of her mother made tangible again.

"Thank you," she said, her eyes misting. "You have no idea what this means to us."

Grayson nodded, unsure of what to say. "I'm just glad I could help."

Lila invited him in, offering coffee and a chance to hear more about Lorraine. She spoke of her mother's love for the forest, her years as a teacher, her insistence on finding beauty even in the smallest things. As Lila talked, Grayson felt a connection to the woman he'd never met, her presence lingering in the room like sunlight filtering through leaves.

The forest began to heal in the weeks that followed. Shoots of green pushed through the blackened soil, a quiet resilience that never ceased to amaze Grayson. He thought of Lorraine often, of the urn and the way it had brought him into her story.

One evening, as the sun dipped below the horizon, he returned to Pine Hollow. The air was cool, carrying the faint scent of new growth. He stood among the charred trees, their silhouettes stark against the fading light, and felt the weight of the past and present converging.

The forest, like Lorraine, was a keeper of memories. And in its quiet mysterious way, it carried them forward, ashes scattered in the wind, life blooming in their wake.

Chapter Seventeen

The Lighthouse Poet

The lighthouse stood at the edge of the world, where the ocean met the cliffs in a violent embrace of salt and stone. Its light, a steady pulse, swept across the sea, its rhythm as familiar as a heartbeat. Inside, the air smelled of brine and aged wood, the walls thick with the stories of those who had come before. It was here, in this solitary beacon, that Evelyn sought refuge from the noise of the world.

She arrived with little more than a suitcase and a stack of notebooks, the latter filled with poems she hadn't read in years. The lighthouse keeper, a grizzled man named Merrick, handed her the keys without ceremony, his eyes narrowing as if trying to decide if she'd last more than a week.

"Storms come fast out here," he warned, his voice rough as the sea air. "The kind that don't just rattle windows. They'll rattle you, too."

Evelyn nodded, though she wasn't entirely sure what he meant. She climbed the winding stairs to the lantern room, her footsteps echoing in the hollow tower. At the top, she gazed out at the vast expanse of water, her breath catching. It was endless, hypnotic, and terrifying. Exactly what she'd been looking for.

The first week passed in relative quiet. Evelyn settled into a routine: mornings spent writing, afternoons walking the cliffs, evenings curled up by the fire with a book. The isolation was both a balm and a burden. She'd fled to the lighthouse to escape—from deadlines, from accolades that felt hollow, from the weight of expectation that had turned her words into something brittle. Here, there was nothing but the sea and her own thoughts.

And then the whispers began.

They came at night, soft at first, like the rustle of pages in an unseen wind. She'd wake to the sound, heart pounding, only to find the room empty, the lantern's light casting long shadows on the walls. By the third night, the whispers grew clearer, forming words she recognized. Words she had written.

Evelyn sat at her desk, staring at the poem she'd been revising. The lines felt stiff, lifeless, as though the ink had dried before the thought had fully formed. She closed the notebook with a frustrated sigh and reached for another, older one. As she flipped through the pages, a chill ran through her. The words were there, but they seemed... different. As if they had rearranged themselves in her absence.

The sea knows the weight of longing.

The line stared back at her, unfamiliar yet undeniably hers. She remembered writing it years ago, during a sleepless night in her tiny apartment, but it hadn't read this way then. The words were sharper now, more urgent, as if the poem had grown teeth.

"You remember," a voice murmured, low and haunting. Evelyn froze, her breath catching in her throat. Slowly, she turned toward the source of the sound.

There, by the window, stood a figure. It was hazy, translucent, as though it were made of smoke and memory. But the eyes were unmistakable. They were hers.

The ghost—if that's what it was—appeared again the next night, and the night after that. It didn't speak much, but its presence was enough. It lingered by the shelves, its fingers tracing the spines of her notebooks, or stood at the desk, staring at the words as though it could read her intentions. Evelyn began to notice other changes, too. Her poems shifted when she wasn't looking, lines vanishing only to reappear in different forms, stanzas rearranging themselves into patterns she hadn't intended but couldn't deny felt right.

The isolation no longer felt comforting. It felt crowded, as though the lighthouse itself had become a vessel for the things she'd tried to leave behind.

One stormy evening, Evelyn sat in the lantern room, the wind howling outside. The ghost stood across from her, its presence heavier than before. She clutched a notebook in her lap, its pages trembling in her hands.

"Why are you here?" she demanded, her voice breaking. "What do you want from me?"

The ghost tilted its head, its expression unreadable. Then it spoke, its voice like the echo of waves in a cavern. "To remind you."

"Of what?" Evelyn's words came out sharper than she intended.

"That the words are not yours to keep. They're meant to be given away."

The weight of the truth settled over her, undeniable. She'd come here to hide, to hoard her words and lock them away. But in doing so, she'd forgotten why she wrote in the first place. Not for recognition, or accolades, but to connect. To offer something of herself to the world, even if it meant being vulnerable.

The next morning, the storm had passed, leaving the air crisp and clear. Evelyn sat at her desk, her pen moving steadily across the page. The ghost was gone, but its presence lingered in the lines she wrote, in the rhythm of the words that flowed freely for the first time in years.

When Merrick returned a week later to check on her, he found her packing her things. "You heading out?" he asked, his tone neutral but curious.

Evelyn nodded, a faint smile on her lips. "I've got work to do."

As she drove away from the lighthouse, the ocean stretched out beside her, endless and full of possibility. And for the first time in a long while, Evelyn felt the same.

Chapter Eighteen

A Taste of Copper

The smell of sweat and old leather still clung to the gym, even after all these years. It hit Len the moment he pushed the door open, a scent so thick it could've been bottled and sold as nostalgia. The place hadn't changed much since he'd last stepped inside—same creaking floorboards, same faded posters peeling off the walls, same heavy bag swaying in the corner like a tired old soldier. He let the door swing shut behind him, the clang of the bell above it echoing in the quiet space.

"You lost, old man?"

The voice came from the ring, where a wiry kid with sharp cheekbones and a mouth too big for his face leaned against the ropes. His gloves dangled from his neck, and the smirk on his lips was the kind that begged for a good right hook.

"Looking for Jimmy," Len said, ignoring the bait.

"He's in the office," the kid replied, jerking his thumb toward the back. "But you might wanna stick around. Show's about to start."

Len grunted and made his way past the ring, the boards creaking under his boots. He could feel the kid's eyes on him, the way he sized him up like a predator gauging the distance to its prey.

Jimmy looked older, though Len supposed that was fair. They both were. The trainer sat behind a desk cluttered with hand wraps and a coffee mug that smelled more like whiskey than caffeine. His face lit up when he saw Len, the lines around his eyes deepening as he smiled.

"Well, I'll be damned," Jimmy said, standing to clasp Len's hand in a grip still strong enough to crush bones. "What brings you back here?"

Len hesitated, the words catching in his throat like they always did. "Saw the poster," he finally said, nodding toward the one taped to the wall.

It was new, the colors bright against the faded decor. Friday Night Fight—The Prodigy vs. The Veteran. The faces on it were unfamiliar, but the kid in the ring was front and center, his cocky grin stretched wide.

"That him?" Len asked.

Jimmy nodded. "Joey. Hell of a fighter. Fast, mean, a little too much mouth for his own good. Reminds me of someone else I used to know."

"Who's the veteran?" Len asked, though he already knew.

Jimmy's smile faltered, just for a second. "I was gonna call you, Len. Honest. But I didn't think you'd wanna step back in the ring."

Len's gut tightened. He hadn't fought in years. Not since the match that ended with the taste of copper flooding his mouth and his knuckles cracking like dry wood against a man who wouldn't stay down. Not since the headlines screamed his name alongside words like "brutal" and "regret."

"I'm not here to fight," Len said, though he wasn't sure if he believed it.

Joey moved like smoke, darting across the ring with a speed that made the air hum. Len watched from the edge, his arms crossed, his jaw tight. The kid's punches snapped like firecrackers, his feet dancing with a rhythm that felt annoyingly familiar. He looked too much like someone Len had faced before—someone whose face still haunted his dreams.

"You here to stare or to teach me something?" Joey called, his grin sharp as broken glass.

"You've got a strong left," Len said. "But you telegraph it. Anyone worth their gloves will see it coming."

Joey's smile faltered. Just a fraction.

"You think you can do better?" the kid challenged, his tone dripping with bravado.

Len's hands clenched at his sides. He'd promised himself he wouldn't do this. Not again. But something about the way Joey moved, the way he taunted, felt like a rope around Len's ribs, pulling him into the past.

"Alright, kid," Len said, stepping through the ropes. "Let's see what you've got."

The first punch came faster than Len expected, a blur that caught him just below the ribs. He staggered, his breath hitching, but he didn't fall. Joey smirked, his gloves raised, bouncing lightly on the balls of his feet.

"You getting slow, old man?" Joey teased.

Len didn't answer. He shifted his weight, his stance lowering as he circled the kid. The ring felt smaller than it used to, the crowd's ghostly cheers ringing in his ears. He waited, his muscles coiled, until Joey moved in again. This time, Len saw it. The telegraphed left. The cocky grin. And he countered, his fist connecting with Joey's side in a punch that rattled the ropes.

The kid's smirk disappeared.

"Not bad," Joey admitted, his voice tight. "You still got it."

"Damn right I do," Len said, wiping sweat from his brow. But the taste of copper lingered in his mouth, the memory of fights won and lost pressing against his ribs.

Later, as Joey slumped against the ropes, chest heaving, he looked at Len with something new in his eyes. Respect, maybe. Or understanding.

"Who was he?" Joey asked. "The guy you're seeing when you look at me."

Len's breath caught. He thought of Tony, the fighter he'd beaten into oblivion all those years ago. The one who'd looked at him afterward with eyes that asked why. The one who'd walked away from the ring and never came back.

"Someone I owe better," Len said, his voice low.

Joey nodded, the fight draining from his posture. "Well, maybe you can pay it forward."

Len looked at the kid, his sharp angles softened by exhaustion, and felt something shift. The ring wasn't just a place for fighting. It was a place for reckoning, for redemption. And maybe, just maybe, it wasn't too late for either.

Chapter Nineteen

The Shadow Cartographer

The boat rocked gently against the dock, its hull weathered from too many journeys across restless seas. Nathan pulled his satchel tighter against his side, his hand brushing the edge of the brass compass that hung from his belt. The island loomed ahead, a jagged silhouette against the early morning sky. It had no name on the maps, just an ominous blank space surrounded by rumors. That was why he'd been hired—to give the uncharted land a shape, a story, and a place in the world.

The air was heavy with the scent of salt and damp earth as he stepped onto the wooden planks of the dock. His guide, a wiry man with sun-beaten skin and a permanent scowl, waited silently. The man offered no introduction, no pleasantries—just a grunt and a nod toward the dense forest that stretched from the shoreline to the peaks beyond.

"What's it called?" Nathan asked, gesturing toward the expanse.

The guide shrugged. "Doesn't have a name. Doesn't need one."

The first day was uneventful. Nathan sketched the coastline, marking the jagged rocks and hidden coves with precision. The forest crept closer with each hour, its shadows long and reaching, as though it were eager to consume the daylight. By the time he set up camp, the sun was low, and the guide had disappeared into the trees without a word.

That night, as Nathan lay beneath a canopy of stars, he noticed the shadows. They stretched and shifted across the ground, independent of the flickering firelight. He rubbed his eyes, blaming exhaustion, but when he looked again, the shadows were gone, folded back into the night.

The next morning, he ventured deeper into the forest, his compass spinning uselessly in his hand. The trees were ancient, their gnarled roots twisting through the soil like the veins of some slumbering giant. The light barely penetrated the canopy, leaving the world below bathed in a muted, greenish haze. As he walked, he couldn't shake the feeling that the shadows were watching him.

By midday, he reached a clearing. In its center stood a rock formation, jagged and unnatural, as though it had been pulled from the earth by unseen hands. He set up his tools, sketching the scene with meticulous care, but as he worked, he noticed something strange. The shadows cast by the rocks didn't align with the sun's position. They moved, fluid and deliberate, as though they had a will of their own.

Nathan's pen faltered, a jagged line marring the pristine page of his notebook. He set it aside, his gaze fixed on the shadows. They seemed to ripple like water, shifting and coalescing into shapes that defied explanation. For a moment, he thought he saw a figure—tall and thin, with eyes that glinted like obsidian.

"The shadows don't belong to you," the guide said that evening, his voice low and gruff. He had returned to the camp, his presence as sudden as his departure.

Nathan looked up from his sketches, his hands trembling. "What does that mean?"

The guide shook his head. "It means you've seen too much. This place isn't meant to be mapped."

"That's why I'm here," Nathan replied, his voice firmer than he felt. "To chart what hasn't been charted. To make sense of it."

The guide's laugh was hollow, humorless. "You can't make sense of shadows. They'll twist your map and your mind until you don't know the difference between the two."

On the third day, Nathan's determination wavered. The forest seemed alive, its shadows growing bolder with each passing hour. They reached for him, curling around his boots, brushing against his hands. He tried to ignore them, focusing on his work, but the unease gnawed at him like a hungry thing.

In the afternoon, he stumbled upon a cavern, its entrance hidden beneath a curtain of moss. The air inside was cool and damp, carrying the faint unusual smell of stone and time. He lit a lantern, its light barely pushing back the darkness, and stepped inside.

The walls were covered in carvings—maps, he realized, etched into the stone with a precision that matched his own. But these maps were wrong. The lines twisted and looped in impossible ways, defying the logic of geography. At their center was an image that made his breath catch: a figure, tall and thin, with eyes like obsidian.

The shadows inside the cavern moved differently. They didn't wait for the light; they existed on their own, shifting and dancing across the walls. As Nathan stared, he felt a pull, a compulsion to step closer, to touch the carvings, to let the shadows claim him.

He fled the cavern, his satchel forgotten, his heart pounding. The guide was waiting for him at the edge of the forest, his expression grim.

"Didn't I warn you?" the guide asked.

Nathan's voice was hoarse, his words tumbling over themselves. "The shadows, the maps... they're alive. They're..."

"They're not yours," the guide interrupted. "Leave this place while you still can."

Nathan didn't finish his map. He left the island the next morning, his compass still spinning, his notebook abandoned in the depths of the forest.

As the boat carried him away, he looked back at the island, its silhouette sharp against the horizon. The shadows were waiting, their presence a promise and a warning.

In the years that followed, Nathan never spoke of the island. But on quiet nights, he felt the pull of its shadows, calling to him from the edges of his memory, reminding him that some places are meant to remain unknown.

Chapter Twenty

Echoes in the Quarry

The quarry stretched out like a scar across the landscape, its jagged edges cutting into the earth as if someone had ripped the terrain apart with their bare hands. Marie stood at the edge, boots caked with red clay, the wind carrying the odor of minerals and damp stone. This place had a voice, she was certain of it. A low hum beneath the surface, like something alive had been buried there and was still trying to be heard.

The formations had drawn her in. Picturesque layers of sedimentary rock folded in ways that defied logic. Strata twisted into spirals and waves, carved not by water or wind but by something more deliberate. It was why she was here, with her notebook and tools, trying to understand how nature had created something so unnatural.

The first sound came as she set up her equipment. A faint vibration, like the quarry itself had exhaled. She froze, her hand on the drill, listening. The wind cut through the silence, followed by the distant cry of a hawk. Then, nothing.

"It's just the wind," she muttered to herself, but the words felt hollow.

By midday, the sun hung heavy above the quarry, turning the rocks into a kaleidoscope of orange and gold. Marie worked methodically, collecting samples, sketching the formations, running her fingers over the ridges to feel their stories. The rocks were warm, their surfaces smooth in some places, jagged in others. They felt... wrong. Not in texture, but in presence, as though they'd been touched by hands far older than time.

It was when she set the drill into the deepest crevice that the ground beneath her shifted. Not much—just a tremor—but enough to send a jolt of adrenaline through her veins. She pulled the drill back and crouched, her palm pressed to the ground. A faint sound reached her ears, too rhythmic to be the natural groan of earth settling. It wasn't a vibration. It was a heartbeat.

The chamber revealed itself just before dusk. The drill had broken through an unexpected hollow, and Marie had widened the opening with careful precision. She shone her flashlight into the darkness, the beam slicing through layers of dust and revealing a staircase carved into the rock. Each step was worn smooth, edges rounded by time.

Marie hesitated. Every rational part of her screamed to mark the spot and call for reinforcements. But the hum beneath her feet had grown louder, resonating in her chest like a song she'd always known but never understood. She couldn't leave. Not yet.

The descent was slow, her footsteps echoing in the narrow tunnel. The air grew cooler, tinged with a unrecognizable taste that made her throat tighten. The flashlight flickered as if it, too, were afraid. And then she reached the chamber.

It was vast, larger than she could have imagined, the ceiling arching high above like the belly of a beast. The walls were covered in carvings, intricate and fluid, depicting scenes she couldn't begin to comprehend. Figures stood in circles, their hands raised toward a central point. Spirals and geometric patterns radiated outward, connecting them in ways that defied logic.

At the center of the room was a pedestal, and atop it, a crystal that pulsed with a faint, amber light. The heartbeat she'd felt earlier was louder here, synchronized with the glow of the crystal. She approached slowly, her breath shallow, her hands trembling.

As her fingers brushed the crystal, the echoes began.

Voices, fragmented and layered, filled the chamber. They spoke in a language she didn't recognize, their tones urgent, pleading. Images flashed before her eyes—a civilization thriving beneath the surface, their lives intertwined with the stone, their technology ancient but impossibly advanced. She saw their fall, a catastrophic event that shattered their world and buried their legacy beneath the earth.

The echoes grew louder, overlapping, threatening to overwhelm her. She stumbled back, her flashlight clattering to the ground. The light flickered wildly, casting the carvings in harsh, shifting shadows. For a moment, she thought she saw one of the figures move.

"Leave," the voices seemed to say, their collective tone not threatening but sorrowful. "Leave and remember."

Marie's chest tightened, her breath coming in short gasps. She scrambled for the flashlight, her fingers brushing the cold metal, and turned it toward the pedestal. The crystal's glow had dimmed, its heartbeat fading into silence.

She climbed out of the quarry as night fell, her legs unsteady, her mind reeling. The chamber's secrets weighed heavy in her thoughts, its echoes still reverberating in her chest. She knew she couldn't explain what she'd found—not in a way anyone would believe. The formations were beyond natural. The chamber beyond human.

Back at her tent, Marie sat with her notebook open, her pen hovering above the page. She wanted to write it all down, to record every detail before it slipped away. But the words felt inadequate, her sketches too crude to capture what she'd seen.

In the end, she wrote only one line: *The earth remembers, even when we forget.*

The quarry slept behind her, its voice quiet for now. But Marie knew its song would call to her again, its echoes waiting for someone willing to listen.

Chapter Twenty-One

The Clockmaker's Confession

The letter arrived on a rainy afternoon, sealed with a smear of wax so dark it might as well have been blood. The envelope bore no return address, only the trembling scrawl of my name across the front. Inside, the parchment was thin and brittle, its edges curling as though it had spent decades trying to escape itself. The words—dense, looping, frantic—belonged to one man: Alaric Maher, the clockmaker.

I hadn't thought of him in years, not since the day he'd shuttered his little shop on the corner of Main and Pine, muttering about hands that refused to turn. But the clock tower—his masterpiece—had loomed over the town square every day of my life, its shadow slicing through the cobblestones like a blade. Its chimes marked the hours, a deep, resonant toll that seemed to vibrate in my very bones.

I unfolded the letter with care, its musty scent curling into my nostrils like a warning.

To whoever finds this—

I am dying. The doctors say it is my heart, but I know better. It is the clock. The weight of it has ground me down, second by second, year by year. I cannot bear its burden any longer, but someone must know the truth.

The tower... it is not what you think it is.

My pulse quickened as I read on, the rain tapping against the window in a rhythm almost too deliberate. Alaric's words unfurled like the gears of one of his creations, intricate and unrelenting. He spoke of the commission he had received three decades ago, a request from the town council to build a clock that would put our sleepy hamlet on the map. He had been young then, ambitious, eager to leave his mark.

But the materials were strange, he wrote. The gears, delivered in unmarked crates, glinted with an unnatural sheen. The pendulum, impossibly heavy, seemed to sway of its own accord, even before it was hung. And the face of the clock...

"It was the eyes," Alaric had scrawled, the ink smudged as though his hand had trembled. "The eyes were watching me."

I thought back to the countless times I'd stood beneath that clock tower, its hands slicing through the sky. I'd never noticed anything unusual about the face, but now, as I pictured it, a shiver ran down my spine. The numbers, the markings—they weren't quite right, were they? They didn't just measure time; they measured something else.

Alaric's letter continued, unraveling into madness. He described the nights he spent alone in the tower, his lantern casting jagged shadows as he assembled the pieces. He spoke of whispers that seemed to emanate from the gears, voices urging him to finish, to seal their fate. And when the clock was finally complete, when its chimes rang out for the first time, he felt it—a pulse, a life.

"It is not a machine," he wrote. "It is a prison. And every tick of its hands is another soul devoured."

I dropped the letter, my hands trembling. The words felt impossible, absurd. Yet as I glanced toward the square, the tower stood there, implacable and silent, its presence suddenly oppressive. The chimes struck four, their toll reverberating through the air like a warning.

I couldn't let it go. That night, armed with a flashlight and a crowbar, I climbed the narrow staircase that spiraled into the clock tower's heart. The air grew colder as I ascended, the smell of oil and rust thickening with each step. When I reached the top, the great gears turned slowly, their teeth interlocking with a precision that felt too perfect. The pendulum swung, its arc impossibly smooth.

In the center of it all was the face of the clock. From the inside, it was even more unsettling. The numbers glowed faintly, their edges too sharp, their forms almost organic. And the hands... they moved not with the steady tick of a mechanism, but with the fluidity of something alive.

I approached the central mechanism, my flashlight trembling in my grip. There, nestled among the gears, was something that didn't belong. A chamber, small and unassuming, its surface etched with symbols that hurt to look at. I pried it open, and inside, I found them—shards of bone, fragments of hair, objects that pulsed with an energy I couldn't comprehend.

The clock struck midnight, and the air seemed to ripple. The whispers Alaric had written of were no longer faint. They surged around me, voices layered upon voices, pleading, screaming, demanding. My flashlight flickered, the beam catching glimpses of things I couldn't name, couldn't face. I stumbled back, the chamber falling shut with a clang that silenced the voices as suddenly as they had begun.

I fled the tower that night, the letter clutched in my hand. I told no one what I'd found, but I couldn't unhear the echoes, couldn't unfeel the weight of the knowledge I now carried. Alaric was right. The clock was a prison. And with every chime, it tightened its grip.

The town still gathers in the square, oblivious to the truth that looms above them. But I know. And every time I hear the chimes, I wonder if it's counting down... or up.

Chapter Twenty-Two

Paper Cranes

The first paper crane was clumsy, its edges creased in all the wrong places. A corner jutted out where it shouldn't have, and the wings were uneven, one shorter than the other. Sam held it up, squinting at the light coming through the window, as if some divine revelation might confirm its worth.

It wasn't perfect, but it was something.

The crane joined a growing flock on the windowsill, a patchwork of pastels from torn construction paper, grocery receipts, and old notebook pages. Each one bore the marks of Sam's hands—smudged ink, fingerprints, tiny tears where the folds had been too sharp. The room smelled faintly of glue and pencil shavings, the air heavy with a silence that had settled in after the funeral.

"You know the story, right?" Uncle Rob had said, crouching down to Sam's level, his knees cracking like brittle wood. "A thousand cranes, one wish."

Sam had nodded, unsure if they believed it but desperate for something to hold on to. The funeral had been a blur—flowers, murmured condolences, and the sound of dirt hitting wood. The cranes were the only thing that made sense, their sharp folds and deliberate creases giving shape to a world that had crumpled in on itself.

The second crane came easier, its wings symmetrical, its beak pointed like an arrow. Sam folded it late at night, the bedside lamp casting long shadows across the room. The quiet hours after everyone else had gone to bed were the worst. The stillness made it harder to ignore the absence, the way the house seemed to sag under the weight of it.

By the third crane, Sam had started to whisper wishes as they folded. Little things at first: I wish for a sunny day tomorrow. I wish I won't trip over my words at school. But as the cranes multiplied, the wishes deepened, the folds carrying the weight of something larger. I wish for one more hug. I wish they weren't gone.

The days bled into weeks, and the cranes began to take over the room. They hung from strings tied to the ceiling, clustered on bookshelves, and lined the edges of the desk. Uncle Rob poked his head in one evening, his eyebrows raising at the sight.

"You're really doing it," he said, stepping inside and picking up one of the cranes. It was made from a piece of graph paper, the blue lines crisscrossing its wings like veins.

Sam shrugged. "You said a thousand, right?"

Rob sat on the edge of the bed, the mattress sinking under his weight. "Yeah, but... I didn't think you'd actually try." He set the crane back down gently, his fingers lingering on its wing. "You miss them a lot, huh?"

Sam's hands stilled, the half-folded crane in their lap suddenly feeling heavier. They nodded, their throat tightening. Rob didn't push, didn't fill the silence with platitudes or advice. He just sat there, the steady rise and fall of his breathing anchoring the room.

By the time the 500th crane joined the flock, Sam had stopped counting. The process had become a ritual, each fold a meditation, each crease a conversation. They imagined the cranes carrying their wishes upward, their paper wings beating against the weight of gravity.

One night, as Sam folded a crane from an old sheet of music, a memory surfaced. It was small and fleeting, like the flash of a firefly, but it burned brightly in the dark. They were sitting on the porch, a cup of hot cocoa warming their hands, listening to the rain drum against the roof.

"It's okay to be sad sometimes," the voice had said, steady and warm. "Sadness means you cared. And caring... that's what makes life beautiful."

Sam's hands faltered, the paper slipping from their grip. They clenched their fists, the words echoing in the quiet room. For the first time since the funeral, the tears came, hot and unrelenting. They poured out in a torrent, drenching the folds they'd so carefully constructed.

The next morning, Sam woke to sunlight streaming through the window, the cranes glowing softly in the golden light. The sadness hadn't vanished, but it had shifted, its edges less jagged. They picked up the damp, crumpled crane from the night before and smoothed it out, their fingers moving with practiced care. It wasn't perfect, but it was something.

As the weeks turned into months, the cranes became more than wishes. They became reminders—of love, of loss, of resilience. Each one carried a piece of the journey, their wings holding the weight of a heart learning to heal.

On the day the thousandth crane joined the flock, Sam stood in the center of the room, their chest tight with something that felt like both grief and gratitude. They didn't make a wish. Instead, they opened the window, the cool breeze rustling the paper wings around them. One by one, they lifted the cranes, releasing them into the sky.

The last crane lingered in their hands, its folds crisp and sharp, its wings steady. Sam whispered a quiet thank you and let it go, watching as it joined the others, their paper wings carrying them higher and higher until they were nothing but specks against the blue.

Chapter Twenty-Three

The Color of Silence

Isaac's studio was a symphony of smells and textures—the sharp smell of turpentine, the buttery smoothness of oil paint, the rough grit of dried canvas beneath his fingertips. He moved through it with an ease that startled visitors, their polite murmurs of disbelief trailing behind him like faint echoes. He didn't need eyes to know where everything was. The brushes sat in jars to his left, sorted by size; the palette lay before him, its surface caked with layers of paint—a tactile roadmap of years spent translating silence into color.

The first painting had been an accident. A canvas left untouched for years, a burst of frustration, and Isaac's hands moving in a desperate rhythm, smearing pigment onto blankness. When it dried, he'd run his fingers over it, feeling the ridges and valleys of the strokes. He didn't need anyone to tell him what it looked like. He could feel it—the tension, the release, the quiet spaces between.

It wasn't long before someone else saw it. Then someone else. Then too many.

"How do you do it?" the journalist asked, her voice carefully modulated, as if speaking too loudly might shatter the moment.

Isaac leaned back in his chair, his hands resting on his lap, flecked with paint.

"How do you explain breathing?" he said, his tone light but edged with exhaustion. "You just do it."

The journalist scribbled something in her notebook, her pen scratching the paper like a faint whisper. Isaac couldn't see her, but he could feel her skepticism. It hung in the air like the smell of rain before a storm.

"But you've never seen color," she pressed. "How do you know what's on the canvas?"

He turned toward her, his face calm, his voice steady. "I don't paint what's seen. I paint what's felt."

The fame came quickly. Too quickly. Galleries filled with his work, critics raving about his ability to capture the ineffable. People stood in front of his paintings for hours, moved to tears by what they couldn't quite name. But with fame came scrutiny, and with scrutiny came questions Isaac couldn't answer.

They wanted to know how he chose his colors, how he layered emotion onto canvas. Some accused him of being a fraud, of letting others do the work while he took the credit. Others insisted on explanations, theories, reasons that could be dissected and analyzed.

"You're trying to box something that doesn't fit," he told them, his frustration barely hidden. "Not everything needs a reason."

The truth was simpler and more complicated than anyone guessed. Isaac's blindness wasn't total. He remembered light, faint and fleeting, like the way the sun felt warm against his skin but disappeared when clouds passed overhead. He remembered colors—not in the way others described them, but as sensations, vibrations that hummed just beneath the surface of his skin.

Blue was the pull of deep water, the ache of longing. Red was sharp and metallic, the taste of blood when you bit your lip. Yellow buzzed like static, relentless and bright. He painted these feelings, layering them one over the other until the canvas vibrated with something he couldn't name but knew to be true.

The backlash hit hardest after the exhibition in New York. A critic had written a scathing piece, accusing Isaac of exploiting his blindness for profit. The words "manipulative" and "fraud" were printed in bold, black ink, their weight pressing down on him like a physical thing.

He'd retreated to his studio, the only place that still felt like his. The brushes waited, the canvas loomed, but his hands trembled too much to begin. The silence pressed in around him, heavier than it had ever been.

It was a letter that broke the silence. A child's handwriting, uneven and sprawling across the page.

Dear Mr. Isaac,

I saw your painting. The one with the swirls. It made me feel like my mom was hugging me, even though she's gone. Thank you.

Isaac traced the words with his fingers, feeling their weight. He folded the letter carefully and set it aside, his hands steady once more.

The next painting was different. Not because of the colors or the technique, but because of the space he left in it. Negative space, the gallery owner called it. But Isaac knew it was more than that. It was room to breathe, room to feel, room for silence to speak.

When it was finished, he ran his hands over the canvas, feeling the story it told. It wasn't perfect, but it was something. And for the first time, that was enough.

Chapter Twenty-Four

The Last Frame

The flea market sprawled across the park in a patchwork of stalls and tarps, a sea of forgotten objects waiting for second chances. The air smelled of fried dough and old wood, and the chatter of haggling voices blended with the faint strains of a street musician's guitar. Claire wandered through the chaos, her camera bag slung over her shoulder, fingers brushing against dusty books and tarnished trinkets as she passed.

She didn't expect to find it. She wasn't looking for anything in particular. But there it was, sitting on a table between a cracked teapot and a stack of vinyl records: an old film camera, its black body scuffed and worn, the lens cap dangling by a frayed strap.

"How much?" she asked, picking it up. It was heavier than it looked, solid and cold against her palms.

The seller, a man with gray stubble and a cigarette balanced on his lip, squinted at her. "Twenty bucks."

Claire hesitated. The thing probably didn't even work, but there was something about it—something that felt like potential.

"Fifteen," she countered.

The man shrugged. "Fine."

Back in her apartment, Claire set the camera on the kitchen table and stared at it while the kettle boiled. It had a name etched into the back in small, precise letters: Chronos 35. She'd never heard of it, but the design was old, probably 1960s or '70s. She popped the back open, half-expecting to find it rusted out or jammed, but it was clean—too clean for something that looked so worn.

There was a roll of film inside, already wound to the first frame. She paused, fingers hovering over the reel. Who left film in a camera they sold? Curiosity prickled at her, and before she could second-guess herself, she grabbed her coat and headed to the darkroom she rented downtown.

The first photograph emerged slowly, the image ghosting onto the paper as she swirled it through the developer. Claire leaned closer, her breath fogging the glass as the picture came into focus.

A man, mid-thirties, with sharp cheekbones and a smile that didn't seem convincing. He was sitting at a diner booth, a cup of coffee in front of him. The background was a blur of neon signs and chrome.

She frowned. She didn't recognize him, and the diner didn't look like anywhere she'd been. The next photo was of a woman standing on a bridge, her scarf caught in the wind, her face turned away from the camera. The third was an empty park bench under a streetlamp, the light pooling like liquid gold on the pavement.

None of it made sense.

Over the next few days, Claire became obsessed. She shot an entire roll of film with the Chronos 35—buildings, strangers, the view from her fire escape—but when she developed the pictures, they weren't hers. The images were of people and places she didn't know: a child chasing pigeons in a plaza, a weathered hand holding a pocket watch, a man in a trench coat stepping onto a train.

By the third roll, the photos began to feel familiar. The people, the settings—they weren't just strangers anymore. They were intersections, fleeting moments she couldn't place but felt like she'd brushed against in passing. A man who might've bumped her shoulder on the subway. A woman she'd glimpsed in line at the grocery store.

And then she saw him.

The photograph was crisp, perfectly framed: a man standing in front of a bookstore, his coat collar turned up against the wind. He was smiling, but it wasn't posed. It was soft, natural, the kind of smile that felt like it belonged to someone you should know.

Claire stared at it for a long time. She didn't know him. She was sure of it. And yet, the sight of his face stirred something in her chest, a quiet ache she couldn't name.

She found him two weeks later.

It happened by accident—or maybe it didn't. She was walking to the darkroom, the camera slung over her shoulder, when she passed the bookstore. It was the same one from the photo, its green awning sagging slightly, a rack of used paperbacks outside. And there he was, standing exactly as he had in the picture, his hands in his pockets, his eyes scanning the street.

Claire froze. The world seemed to narrow, the sounds of the city fading into the background. She wanted to approach him, to say something, but what? Hey, I developed your photograph before I met you. Want to grab coffee?

Before she could decide, he turned and walked away, disappearing into the crowd.

The next photo was of her.

She found it three days later, buried at the end of the roll she'd just developed. It was unmistakable: her face, her apartment, the faint smudge of sunlight filtering through the curtains. She felt the blood drain from her cheeks. She hadn't taken it. No one else had been in her apartment.

The Chronos 35 sat on her desk, quiet and unassuming. Claire picked it up, her hands trembling, and looked through the viewfinder. The world outside her window came into focus, ordinary and sharp. But when she clicked the shutter, she couldn't shake the feeling that the camera wasn't just recording what it saw. It was showing her what she hadn't yet lived.

Chapter Twenty-Five

Under the Iron Bridge

The city, like most cities, never truly slept. Even in its quietest hours, there was always the hum of something alive beneath its skin. Lila knew this better than most. The bridges, the tunnels, the places where the concrete ended and the shadows began—these were her beats. Her editor called it "the gritty side of investigative journalism." Lila called it "home."

The Iron Bridge had been her focus for weeks. A massive relic of another time, it spanned the river like a rusted spine, holding up the weight of commuters who barely glanced at it as they passed overhead. It was beneath the bridge, in the web of supports and graffiti-streaked girders, that the whispers began. A body had been found in the river nearby years ago, the case unsolved, the story faded into the city's collective amnesia. Lila wasn't the first journalist to chase its ghost, but she was determined to be the last.

Her first visit under the bridge was unremarkable. The air was heavy with the unmistakable smell of river mud, the ground littered with the debris of lives lived out of sight. Empty bottles, torn blankets, charred remains of fires long extinguished. The graffiti told its own stories, a chaotic blend of desperation and defiance. She snapped photos, jotted notes, and left feeling like she'd found nothing but echoes.

It was on her second visit that she saw the light.

The glow was faint, flickering like a candle in a drafty room. It came from deeper under the bridge, past the piles of rubble and the remnants of old encampments. Lila hesitated, her instincts warring with her curiosity. Then she heard it: a low murmur, the unmistakable rhythm of human voices. She slipped her phone into her pocket, gripping her flashlight tightly as she moved closer.

The space opened up suddenly, a hidden pocket beneath the bridge's supports. The light came from lanterns strung on wires, casting a warm, golden glow that felt out of place in the cold, industrial void. And there were people—dozens of them. Men, women, even a few children, their faces wary but not hostile as they turned to watch her.

"You're lost," a man said, stepping forward. He was tall and lean, his clothes patched but clean, his eyes sharp and steady.

"Not exactly," Lila replied, raising her hands in a gesture of peace. "I'm a journalist. My name's Lila."

The man's expression didn't change. "We don't need a story. We need to be left alone."

Over the next few days, Lila returned to the bridge, each time lingering a little longer. She brought small offerings—food, blankets, first-aid supplies—and asked no questions. The community, as she began to think of them, was wary but not unkind. They called the man who had spoken to her Miles. He seemed to be their leader, though not by design. Leadership here wasn't about power; it was about trust.

"We came here because there was nowhere else," Miles told her one evening. They were sitting by one of the fires, its smoke curling into the shadows above. "The city forgot about this place. About us. So we built something for ourselves."

Lila nodded, her pen hovering over her notebook. "And the body in the river? Was that someone from here?"

Miles' jaw tightened. "You don't get it. The city's problems aren't our problems. We didn't kill anyone. But that doesn't stop them from blaming us."

The deeper Lila delved, the more she began to see the city's underbelly not as a place of crime and decay but as a patchwork of resilience. The community under the Iron Bridge wasn't a monolith. There were those who had fled abuse, those who had slipped through the cracks of a broken system, and those who simply wanted to disappear. They weren't criminals. They were survivors.

But the body in the river still hung over everything. The police had written it off as a vagrant's misfortune. Lila wasn't so sure. The more she learned about the community, the more it seemed like they were protecting something. Or someone.

It was Miles who finally told her the truth. They were sitting on the edge of the river, the bridge looming above them, its shadow stretching across the water.

"It was an accident," he said quietly. "The guy was drunk. Started a fight. Fell. Nobody pushed him, but... nobody tried to stop it, either."

Lila's pen stilled. "Why didn't you tell the police?"

Miles laughed bitterly. "You think they'd believe us? We're ghosts to them. Less than ghosts. They'd have torn this place apart looking for someone to blame."

She couldn't argue with that. The city had always turned a blind eye to the people under its bridges, except when it needed someone to blame.

The story Lila wrote wasn't about the crime. It was about the community—their struggles, their resilience, their humanity. She wrote about the lives they'd built in the shadows and the way the city had failed them. And when it was published, it didn't solve anything. The city didn't suddenly wake up and fix its problems. But it made people look. It made them see.

Lila still visits the Iron Bridge sometimes. She brings supplies, shares stories, and sits by the fires with people who have become more than sources. And when she walks away, the city feels different, its hum a little quieter, its shadows a little less heavy.

Epilogue

The stories in this collection are complete, yet their echoes remain. They ripple outward, connecting with the stories we carry in ourselves. Perhaps you've recognized a fragment of your own life within these pages—a familiar ache, a fleeting joy, a lingering question. That's the beauty of storytelling: it bridges the gaps between us, reminding us that we're never truly alone. As you close this book, I hope you carry these stories with you, not as endings but as beginnings of conversations yet to come.

Afterword

Every story begins with a question: What if? What lies beyond the edges of what we know? As I wrote these stories, I realized that the answers are never simple. They unfold in layers, in whispers, in the spaces between what is said and what is left unsaid. The characters in these pages—the blind painter, the grieving child, the lighthouse poet—all wrestle with these questions in their own ways, and their struggles have become my own. I hope these tales linger with you as they have with me, sparking curiosity and a deeper appreciation for the complexities of the human experience.

Made in the USA
Columbia, SC
27 December 2024

50742045R00065